The Crimson Circle

Edgar Wallace

DODO PRESS

The Crimson Circle

by

Edgar Wallace

PROLOGUE

THE NAIL

IT is a ponderable fact that had not the 29th of a certain September been the anniversary of Monsieur Victor Pallion's birth, there would have been no Crimson Circle mystery; a dozen men, now dead, would in all probability be alive, and Thalia Drummond would certainly never have been described by a dispassionate inspector of police as "a thief and the associate of thieves."

M. Pallion entertained his three assistants to dinner at the Coq d'Or in the city of Toulouse, and the proceedings were both joyous and amiable. At three o'clock in the morning it dawned upon M. Pallion that the occasion of his visit to Toulouse was the execution of an English malefactor named Lightman.

"My children," he said gravely but unsteadily, "it is three hours and the 'red lady' has yet to be assembled!"

So they adjourned to the place before the prison where a trolley containing the essential parts of the guillotine had been waiting since midnight, and with a skill born of practice they erected the grisly thing, and fitted the knife into its proper slots.

But even mechanical skill is not proof against the heady wines of southern France, and when they tried the knife it did not fall truly.

"I will arrange this," said M. Pallion, and drove a nail into the frame at exactly the place where a nail should not have been driven.

But he was getting flurried, for the soldiers had marched on to the ground..

Four hours later (it was light enough for an enterprising photographer to snap the prisoner close at hand), they inarched a man from the prison..

"Courage!" murmured M. Pallion.

"Go to hell!" said the victim, now lying strapped upon the plank.

M. Pallion pulled a handle and the knife fell as far as the nail. Three times he tried and three times he failed, and then the indignant spectators broke through the military cordon, and the prisoner was taken back into the gaol. Eleven years later that nail killed many people.

CHAPTER I

THE INITIATION

IT was an hour when most respectable citizens were preparing for bed, and the upper windows of the big, old-fashioned houses in the square showed patches of light, against which the outlines of the leafless trees, bending and swaying under the urge of the gale, were silhouetted. A cold wind was sweeping up the river, and its outriders penetrated icily into the remotest and most sheltered places.

The man who paced slowly by the high iron railings shivered, though he was warmly clad, for the unknown had chosen a rendezvous which seemed exposed to the full blast of the storm.

The debris of the dead autumn whirled in fantastic circles about his feet, the twigs and leaves came rattling down from the trees which threw their long gaunt arms above him, and he looked enviously at the cheerful glow in the windows of a house where, did he but knock, he would be received as a welcome guest.

The hour of eleven boomed out from a nearby clock, and the last stroke was reverberating when a car came swiftly and noiselessly into the square and halted abreast of him. The two head-lamps burned dimly. Within the closed body there was no spark of light. After a moment's hesitation the waiting man stepped to the car, opened the door, and got in. He could only guess the outline of the driver's figure in the seat ahead, and he felt a curious thumping of heart as he realised the terrific importance of the step he had taken. The car did not move, and the man in the driver's seat remained motionless. For a little time there was a dead silence, which was broken by the passenger.

"Well?" he asked nervously, almost irritably.

"Have you decided?" asked the driver.

"Should I be here if I hadn't?" demanded the passenger. "Do you think I've come out of curiosity? What do you want of me? Tell me that, and I will tell you what I want of you."

"I know what you want of me," said the driver. His voice was muffled and indistinct, as one who spoke behind a veil.

When the newcomer's eyes grew accustomed to the gloom, he detected the vague outline of the black silk cowl which covered the driver's head.'

"You are on the verge of bankruptcy," the driver went on. "You have used money which was not yours to use, and you are contemplating suicide. And it is not your insolvency which makes you consider this way out. You have an enemy who has discovered something to your discredit, something which would bring you into the hands of the police. Three days ago you obtained from a firm of manufacturing chemists, a member of which is a friend of yours, a particularly deadly drug, which cannot be obtained from a retail chemist. You have spent a week reading up poisons and their effects, and it is your intention, unless something turns up which will save you from ruin, to end your life either on Saturday or Sunday. I think it will be Sunday." He heard the man behind him gasp, and laughed softly. "Now, sir," said the driver, "are you prepared for a consideration to act for me?"

"What do you want me to do?" demanded the man behind him shakily.

"I ask no more than that you should carry out my instructions. I will take care that you run no risks and that you are well paid. I am prepared at this moment to place in your hands a very large sum of money, which will enable you to meet your more pressing obligations. In return for this I shall want you to put into circulation all the money I send you, to make the necessary exchanges, to cover up the trail of bills and bank-notes, the numbers of which are known to the police; to dispose of bonds, which I cannot dispose of, and generally to act as my agent—" he paused, adding significantly, "and to pay on demand what I ask."

The man behind him did not reply for some time, and then he asked with a hint of petulance; "What is the Crimson Circle?"

"You," was the startling reply.

"I?" gasped the man.

"You are of the Crimson Circle," said the other carefully. "You have a hundred comrades, none of whom will ever be known to you, none of whom will ever know you."

"And you?"

"I know them all," said the driver. "You agree?"

"I agree," said the other after a pause. The driver half-turned in his seat and held out his hand.

"Take this," he said. "This" was a large, bulky envelope, and the newly initiated member of the Crimson Circle thrust it into his pocket.

"And now get out," said the driver curtly, and the man obeyed without question.

He slammed the door behind him and walked abreast of the driver. He was still curious as to his identity, and for his own salvation it was necessary that he should know the man who drove.

"Don't light your cigar here," said the driver, "or I shall think that your smoking is really an excuse to strike a match. And remember this, my friend, that the man who knows me, carries his knowledge to hell."

Before the other could reply the car moved on and the man with the envelope stood watching its red tail light until it disappeared from view.

He was shaking from head to foot, and when he did light the cigar which his chattering teeth gripped, the flame of the match quivered tremulously.

"That is that," he said huskily, and crossed the road, to disappear in one of the side-turnings. He was scarcely out of sight before a figure moved stealthily from the doorway of a dark house and followed. It was the figure of a man tall and broad, and he walked with difficulty, for he was naturally short of breath. He had gone a hundred paces in his pursuit before he realised that he still held in his hand the ship's binoculars through which he had been watching.

When he reached the main street his quarry had vanished.

He had expected as much and was not perturbed. He knew where to find him. But who was in the car? He had read the number and could trace its owner in the morning. Mr. Felix Marl grinned. Had he so much as guessed the character of the interview he had overlooked, he would not have been amused. Stronger men than he had grown stiff with fear at the menace of the Crimson Circle.

CHAPTER II

THE MAN WHO DID NOT PAY

PHILIP BASSARD paid, and lived, for apparently the Crimson Circle kept faith; Jacques Rizzi, the banker, also paid, but in a panic. He died from natural causes a month later, having a weak heart. Benson, the railway lawyer, pooh-poohed the threat and was found dead by the side of his private saloon.

Mr. Derrick Yale, with his amazing gifts, ran down the coloured man who had crept into Benson's private car and killed him before he threw the body from the window, and the coloured man was hanged, without, however, revealing the identity of his employer. The police might sneer at Yale's psychometrical powers—as they did—but within forty-eight hours he had led the police to the criminal's house at Yareside and the dazed murderer had confessed.

Following this tragedy many men must have paid without reporting the matter to the police, for there was a long period during which no reference to the Crimson Circle found its way into the newspapers. And then one morning there came to the breakfast table of James Beardmore, a square envelope containing a card, on which was stamped a Crimson Circle.

"You are interested in the melodrama of life, Jack—read that."

James Stamford Beardmore tossed the message across the table to his son and proceeded to open the next letter in the pile which stood beside his plate.

Jack retrieved the message from the floor, where it had fallen, and examined it with a little frown. It was a very ordinary letter-card, save that it bore no address. A big circle of crimson touched its four edges, and had the appearance of having been printed with a rubber stamp, for the ink was unevenly distributed. In the centre of the circle, written in printed characters, were the words:

"One hundred thousand represents only a small portion of your possessions. You will pay this in notes to a messenger I will send in response to an advertisement in the Tribune within the next twenty-four hours, stating the exact hour convenient to you. This is the final warning."

There was no signature.

"Well?" Old Jim Beardmore looked up over his spectacles and his eyes were smiling.

"The Crimson Circle!" gasped his son.

Jim Beardmore laughed aloud at the concern in the boy's voice.

"Yes, the Crimson Circle—I have had four of 'em!"

The young man stared at him. "Four?" he repeated. "Good heavens! Is that why Yale has been staying with us?"

Jim Beardmore smiled.

"That is a reason," he said.

"Of course, I knew that he was a detective, but I hadn't the slightest idea—"

"Don't worry about this infernal circle," interrupted his father a little impatiently. "I'm not scared of them. Froyant is in terror of his life that he will be marked down. And I don't wonder. He and I have made a few enemies in our time."

James Beardmore, with his hard, lined face and his stubbly grey beard, might have been mistaken for the grandfather of the good-looking young man who sat opposite to him. The Beardmore fortune had been painfully won. It had materialised from the wreckage of dreams and had its beginnings in the privations, the dangers and the heartaches of a prospector's life. This man whom Death had stalked on the waterless plains of the Kalahari, who had scraped in the mud of the Vale River for illusory diamonds, and thawed out his claim in the Klondyke, had faced too many real dangers to be greatly disturbed by the threat of the Crimson Circle. For the moment his perturbation was based on a more tangible peril, not to himself, but to his son.

"I've got a whole lot of faith in your good sense, Jack," he said, "so don't be hurt by anything I'm going to say. I've never interfered in your amusements or questioned your judgment—but—do you think that you're being wise just now?"

Jack understood. "You mean about Miss Drummond, father?"

The older man nodded.

"She's Froyant's secretary," began the youth.

"I know she is Froyant's secretary," said the other, "and she's none the worse for that. But the point is, Jack, do you know anything more about her?"

The young man rolled his napkin deliberately. His face was red and there was a queer set look about his jaw which secretly amused Jim.

"I like her. She is a friend of mine. I've never made love to her, if that is what you mean, dad, and I rather think our friendship would be at an end if I did."

Jim nodded. He had said all that was necessary and now he took up a more bulky envelope and looked at it curiously. Jack saw that it bore French postage stamps and wondered who was the correspondent.

Tearing open the flap, the old man took out a pad of correspondence, which included yet another envelope heavily sealed. He read the superscription and his nose wrinkled.

"Ugh!" he said, and put the envelope down unopened. He glanced through the remainder of the correspondence, then looked across at his son.

"Never trust a man or woman until you know the worst of them," he said. "I've got a man coming to see me to-day who is a respectable member of society. He has a record as black as my hat and yet I'm going to do business with him—I know the worst!"

Jack laughed. Further conversation was interrupted by the arrival of their guest.

"Good morning, Yale—did you sleep well?" asked the old man. "Ring for some more coffee, Jack."

Derrick Yale's visit had been an unmixed pleasure to Jack Beardmore. He was at the age when romance had its full appeal and the companionship of the most commonplace detective would have brought him a peculiar joy. But the glamour which surrounded Yale was the glamour of the supernatural. This man had unusual and peculiar qualities which made him unique. The delicate aesthetic face, the grave mystery of his eyes, the very gesture of his long, sensitive hands, were part of his uniqueness.

"I never sleep," he said good-humouredly as he unrolled his serviette. He held the silver napkin ring for a second between his two fingers, and James Beardmore watched him with amusement. As for Jack, his eager admiration was unconcealed.

"Well?" asked the old man.

"Who handled this last has had very bad news—some near relation is desperately ill."

Beardmore nodded.

"Jane Higgins was the servant who laid the table," he said. "She had a letter this morning saying that her mother was dying."

Jack gasped.

"And you felt that in the serviette ring?" he asked in amazement. "How do you get that impression, Mr. Yale?"

Derrick Yale shook his head.

"I don't attempt to explain," he said quietly. "All that I know is that the moment I took up my serviette I had a sensation of profound and poignant sorrow. It is weird, isn't it?"

"But how did you know about her mother?"

"I traced it somehow," said the other almost brusquely; "it is a matter of deduction. Have you any news, Mr. Beardmore?"

For answer Jim handed him the card he had received that morning. Yale read the message, then weighed the card on the palm of his white hand.

"Posted by a sailor," he said, "a man who has been in prison and has recently lost a great deal of money."

Jim Beardmore laughed.

"Which I shall certainly not replace," he said, rising from the table. "Do you take these warnings seriously?"

"I take them very seriously," said Derrick in his quiet way. "So seriously that I do not advise you to leave this house except in my company. The Crimson Circle," he went on, arresting Beardmore's indignant protest with a characteristic gesture, "is, I admit, vulgarly melodramatic in its operations, but it will be no solace to your heirs to learn that you have died theatrically."

Jim Beardmore was silent for a time, and his son regarded him anxiously.

"Why don't you go abroad, father?" he asked, and the old man snapped round on him.

"Go abroad be damned!" he roared. "Run away from a cheap Black Hand gang? I'll see them—!"

He did not mention their destination, but they could guess.

CHAPTER III

THE GIRL WHO WAS INDIFFERENT

A HEAVY weight lay on Jack Beardmore's mind as he walked slowly across the meadows that morning. His feet carried him instinctively in the direction of the little valley which lay a mile from the house, and in the exact centre of which ran the hedge which marked the division between the Beardmore and Froyant estates. It was a glorious morning. The storm of wind and rain which had swept the country the night before had blown itself out, and the world lay bathed in yellow sunlight. Far away, beyond the olive-green covens that crowned Penton Hill, he caught a glimpse of Harvey Froyant's big white mansion. Would she venture out with the ground so sodden and the grasses soaked with rain, he wondered?

He stopped by a big elm tree on the lip of the valley and cast an anxious glance along the untidy hedge, until his eyes rested on a tiny summer house which the former owners of Tower House had erected—Harvey Froyant, who loathed solitude, would never have been guilty of such extravagance.

There was nobody in sight, and his heart sank. Ten minutes' walking brought him to the gap he had made in the fence, and he stepped through. The girl who sat in the tiny house might have heard his sigh of relief.

She looked round, then rose with some evidence of reluctance.

She was remarkably pretty, with her fair hair and flawless skin, but there was no welcome in her eyes as she came slowly toward him. "Good morning," she said coolly.

"Good morning, Thalia," he ventured, and her frown returned.

"I wish you wouldn't," she said, and he knew that she meant what she said. Her attitude toward him puzzled and worried him. For she was a thing of laughter and bubbling life. He had once surprised her chasing a hare, and had watched, spellbound, the figure of this laughing Diana as her little feet flew across the field in pursuit of the scared beast. He had heard her singing, too, and the very joy of life was vibrant in her voice—but he had seen her so depressed and gloomy that he had feared she was ill.

"Why are you always so stiff and formal with me?" he grumbled.

For a second a ghost of a smile showed at the comer of her mouth.

"Because I've read books," she said solemnly, "and poor girl secretaries who aren't stiff and formal with millionaire's sons usually come to a bad end!"

She had a trick of directness which was very disconcerting.

"Besides," she said, "there is no reason why I shouldn't be stiff and formal. It is the conventional attitude which people adopt toward their fellow creatures, unless they are very fond of them, and I'm not very fond of you."

She said this calmly and deliberately, and the young man's face went red. He felt a fool, and cursed himself for provoking this act of cruelty.

"I will tell you something, Mr. Beardmore," she went on in her even tone. "Something which you haven't realised. When a boy and girl are thrown together on a desert island, it is only natural that the boy gets the idea that the girl is the only girl in the world. All his wayward fancies are concentrated on one woman and as the days pass she grows more and more wonderful in his eyes. I've read a lot of these desert island stories, and I've seen a lot of pictures that deal with that interesting situation, and that is how it strikes me. You are on a desert island here—you spend too much time on your estate, and the only things you see are rabbits and birds and Thalia Drummond. You should go into the city and into the society of people of your own station."

She turned from him with a nod, for she had seen her employer approaching, had watched him out of the corner of her eye as he stopped to survey them, and had guessed his annoyance.

"I thought you were doing the house accounts, Miss Drummond," he said with asperity.

He was a skinny man, in the early fifties, colourless, sharp-featured, prematurely bald. He had an unpleasant habit of baring his long yellow teeth when he asked a question, a grimace which in some curious way suggested his belief that the answer would be an evasion.

"Morning, Beardmore," he jerked the salutation grudgingly and turned again to his secretary.

"I don't like to see you wasting your time, Miss Drummond," he said.

"I am not wasting either your time or mine, Mr. Froyant," she answered calmly. "I have finished the accounts—here!" She tapped the worn leather portfolio which was under her arm.

"You could have done the work in my library," he complained; "there is no need to go into the wilderness."

He stopped and rubbed his long nose and glanced from the girl to the silent young man.

"Very good; that will do," he said. "I am going to see your father, Beardmore. Perhaps you will walk with me?"

Thalia was already on her way to Tower House, and Jack had no excuse for lingering.

"Don't occupy that girl's time, Beardmore, don't, please," said Froyant testily. "You've no idea how much she has to do—and I'm sure your father wouldn't like it."

Jack was on the point of saying something offensive, but checked himself. He loathed Harvey Froyant, and at the moment hated him for his domineering attitude toward the girl.

"That class of girl," began Mr. Froyant, turning to walk by the side of the hedge toward the gate at the end of the valley, "that class of girl—" he stood still and stared. "Who the devil has broken through the hedge?" he demanded, pointing with his stick.

"I did," said Jack savagely. "It is our hedge, anyway, and it saves half a mile—come on, Mr. Froyant."

Harvey Froyant made no comment as he stepped gingerly through the hedge.

They walked slowly up the hill toward the big elm tree where Jack and stood looking down into the valley.

Mr. Harvey Froyant preserved a tight-lipped silence. He was a stickler for the conventions, where their observations benefited himself.

They had reached the crest of the rise, when suddenly his arm was gripped, and he turned to see Jack Beardmore, staring at the bole of the tree. Froyant followed the direction of his eye and took a step backward, his unhealthy face a shade paler. Painted on the tree trunk was a rough circle of crimson, and the paint was yet wet.

CHAPTER IV

MR. FELIX MARL

JACK BEARDMORE looked round, scanning the country. The only human being in sight was a man who was walking slowly away from them, carrying a bag in his hand. Jack shouted, and the man turned.

"Who are you?" demanded Jack. Then, "What are you doing here?"

The stranger was a tall, stoutish man, and the exertion of carrying his grip had left him a little breathless. It was some time before he could reply.

"My name is Marl," he said, "Felix Marl. You may have heard of me. I think you are young Mr. Beardmore, aren't you?"

"That is my name," said Jack. "What are you doing here?" he asked again.

"They told me there was a short cut from the railway station, but it is not so short as they promised," said Mr. Marl, breathing stertorously. "I'm on my way to see your father."

"Have you been near that tree?" asked Jack, and Marl glared at him.

"Why should I go near any tree?" he demanded aggressively. "I tell you I've come straight across the fields."

By this time Harvey Froyant arrived, and apparently recognised the newcomer.

"This is Mr. Marl; I know him. Marl, did you see anybody near that tree?"

The man shook his head. Apparently the tree and its secret was a mystery to him.

"I never knew there was a tree there," he said. "What—what has happened?"

"Nothing," said Harvey Froyant sharply.

They came to the house soon after, Jack carrying the visitor's bag. He was not impressed by the big man's appearance. His voice was coarse, his manner familiar, and Jack wondered what association this uncouth specimen of humanity could have with his father.

They were nearing the house when suddenly and for no obvious reason the stout Mr. Marl emitted a frightened squeal and leapt back. There was no doubt of his fear. It was written visibly in the blanched cheeks and the quivering lips of the man, who was shaking from head to foot. Jack could only look at him in astonishment—and even Harvey Froyant was startled into an interest.

"What the hell is wrong with you, Marl?" he asked savagely.

His own nerves were on edge, and the sight of the big man's undisguised terror was a further strain which he could scarcely endure.

"Nothin'—nothin'," muttered Marl huskily. "I've been—"

"Drinking, I should think," snapped Froyant.

After seeing the man into the house Jack hurried off in search of Derrick Yale. He discovered the detective in the shrubbery sitting in a big cane chair, his chin upon his breast, his arms folded, a characteristic attitude of his. Yale looked up at the sound of the young man's footsteps. "I can't tell you," he said, before Jack had framed his question, and then, seeing the look of astonishment on his face, he laughed. "You were going to ask me what scared Marl, weren't you?"

"I came with that intention," laughed Jack. "What an extraordinary fellow you are, Mr. Yale! Did you see his extraordinary exhibition of funk?"

Derrick Yale nodded. "I saw him just before he had his shock," he said. "You can see the field path from here." He frowned. "He reminds me of somebody," he said slowly, "yet I cannot for the life of me tell who it is. Is he a frequent visitor here? Your father told me he was coming, and I guessed it was he."

Jack shook his head. "This is the first time I've seen him," he said. "I remember now, though, that father and Froyant have had some business dealings with a man named Marl—Dad mentioned him one day. I think he is a land speculator. Father is rather interested in land just now. By the way, I have seen the mark of the Crimson Circle," he added, and described the newly-painted "O" he had found on the elm. Instantly Yale lost interest in Mr. Marl. "It was not on the tree when I went down into the valley," said Jack. "I'll swear to that. It must have been painted whilst I was talking to—to a friend. The trunk is out of sight from the boundary fence, and it was quite possible for somebody to have painted the sign without being seen. What does it mean, Mr. Yale?"

"It means trouble," said Yale shortly. He rose abruptly and began pacing the flagged walk, and Jack, after waiting a little while, left him to his meditations.

In the meantime, Mr. Felix Marl was comparatively a useless third of a conference which dealt with the transfer of lands. Marl was, as Jack had said, a land speculator, and he had come that morning bringing a promising proposition which he was wholly incapable of explaining.

"I can't help it, gentlemen," he said, and for the fourth time his trembling hand rose to his lips. "I've had a bit of a shock this morning."

"What was that?"

But Marl seemed incapable of explanation. He could only shake his head helplessly. "I'm not fit to discuss things calmly," he said. "You'll have to put the matter off until to-morrow."

"Do you think I've come here to-day for the purpose of listening to that sort of nonsense?" snarled Mr. Froyant. "I tell you I want this business settled. So do you, Beardmore."

Jim Beardmore, who was indifferent as to whether the matter was settled then or the following week, laughed.

"I don't know that it is very important," he said. "If Mr. Marl is upset, why should we bother him? Perhaps you'll stay here to-night. Marl?"

"No, no, no," the man's voice rose almost to a shout. "No, I won't stay here, if you don't mind—I would much rather not!"

"Just as you like," said Jim Beardmore indifferently, and folded up the papers he had prepared for signature.

They walked out into the hall together, and there Jack found them.

Beardmore's car carried the visitor and his bag back to the station, and from there on Mr. Marl's conduct was peculiar. He registered his bag through to the city, but he himself descended at the next station, and for a man who so disliked walking, and as by nature so averse from physical exercise, he displayed an almost heroic spirit, for he set forth to walk the nine miles which separated him from the Beardmore estate—and he did not go by the shortest route.

It was nearing nightfall when Mr. Marl made his furtive way into a thick plantation on the edge of the Beardmore property.

He sat down, a tired, dusty but determined man, and waited for the night to close down over the countryside. And during the period of waiting, he examined with tender care the heavy automatic pistol he had taken from his bag in the train.

CHAPTER V

THE GIRL WHO RAN

"I CAN'T understand why that fellow hasn't come back this morning," said Jim Beardmore with a frown.

"Which fellow?" asked Jack carelessly.

"I'm speaking of Marl," said his father.

"Was that the large-sized gentleman I saw yesterday?" asked Derrick Yale.

They were standing on the terrace of the house, which, from its elevated position, gave them a view across the country.

The morning train had come and gone. They could see the trail of white smoke it left as it disappeared into the foothills nine miles away.

"Yes. I'd better 'phone Froyant, and tell him not to come over."

Jim Beardmore stroked his stubbly chin.

"Marl puzzles me," he said "He is a brilliant fellow I believe, a reformed thief I know—at least I hope he is reformed. What upset him yesterday, Jack? He came into the library looking like death."

"I haven't the slightest idea," said Jack. "I think he has a weak heart, or something of the sort. He told me he gets these spasms occasionally."

Beardmore laughed softly, and going into the house returned with a walking-stick.

"I'm going for a stroll, Jack. No, you needn't come along. I've one or two things I wish to think out, and I promise you, Yale, I won't leave the grounds, though I think you attach too much importance to the threats of these ruffians."

Yale shook his head.

"What of the sign on the tree?" he asked.

Jim Beardmore snorted contemptuously.

"It will take more than that to extract a hundred thousand from me," he said.

He waved a farewell at them as he went down the broad stone steps, and they watched him walking slowly across the park.

"Do you really think my father is in any kind of danger?" asked Jack.

Yale, who had been staring after the figure, turned with a start.

"In danger?" he repeated, and then after a second's hesitation. "Yes, I believe there is very serious danger for him in the next day or two."

Jack turned his troubled gaze upon the disappearing figure.

"I hope you're wrong," he said. "Father doesn't seem to take the matter as seriously as you."

"That is because your father has not the same experience," said the detective, "but I understand that he saw Chief Inspector Parr, and the inspector thought there was considerable danger."

Jack chuckled in spite of his fears.

"How do the lion and the lamb amalgamate?" he asked. "I didn't think that head-quarters had much use for private men like you, Mr. Yale?"

"I admire Parr," said Derrick slowly. "He's slow, but thorough. I am told that he is one of the most conscientious men at head-quarters, and I fancy that the headquarters chiefs have treated him badly over the last Crimson Circle crime. They have practically told him that if he cannot run the organisation to earth he must send in his resignation."

Whilst they were speaking, the figure of Mr. Beardmore had disappeared into the gloom of a little wood on the edge of the estate.

"I worked with him during the last Circle murder," Derrick Yale went on, "and he struck me—"

He stopped, and the two men looked at one another.

There was no mistaking the sound. It was a shot near and distinct, and it came from the direction of the wood. In an instant Jack had leapt over the balustrade and was racing across the meadow. Derrick Yale behind him.

Twenty paces along the woodland path they found Jim Beardmore lying on his face, and he was quite dead, and even as Jack was staring down at his father with horrified eyes, a girl emerged from the wood at the farther end, and stopping only long enough to wipe with a handful of grass something that was red from her hands, she flew along the shadow of the hedge which divided the Froyant estate.

Never once did Thalia Drummond look back until she reached the shelter of the little summer house. Her face was drawn and white, and her breath came gaspingly as she stood for a second in the doorway of the little hut, and looked back to the wood. A swift glance round and she was in the house and on her knees tugging with quivering hands at the end of a floor board. It came up disclosing a black cavity. Another second's hesitation, and she threw into the hole the revolver she had held in her hand, and dropped the board back in its place.

CHAPTER VI

THALIA DRUMMOND IS A CROOK

THE Commissioner looked down at the newspaper cutting before him and tugged at his grey moustache. Inspector Parr, who knew the signs, watched with an apparently detached interest.

He was a short, thick-set man, so lacking in inches that it was remarkable that he had ever satisfied the stringent requirements of the police authorities. His age was something below fifty, but his big red face was unlined. It was a face from whence every indication of intelligence and refinement was absent. The round, staring eyes were bovine in their lack of expression, the big fleshy nose, the heavy cheeks, pouched beneath the jaws, and the half-bald head, were units of his unimpressiveness. The Commissioner picked up the cutting. "Listen to this," he said curtly, and read. It was the editorial of the Morning Monitor and it was direct to a point of offensiveness.

"For the second time during the past year the country has been shocked and outraged by the assassination of a prominent man. It is not necessary to give here the details of this Crimson Circle crime, particulars of which appear on another page. But it is very necessary that we should state in emphatic and unmistakable terms that we view with consternation the seeming helplessness of police headquarters to deal with this criminal gang. Inspector Parr, who has devoted himself for the past year to tracking the murdering blackmailers, can offer us nothing more than vague promises of revelations which never materialise. It is obvious that police headquarters needs a thorough overhauling, and the introduction of new blood, and we trust that those responsible for the government of the country, will not hesitate to make the drastic changes which are necessary."

"Well," growled Colonel Morton, "what do you think of that, Parr?"

Mr. Parr rubbed his big chin and said nothing.

"James Beardmore was murdered after due warning had been given to the police," said the Commissioner deliberately. "He was shot within sight of his house, and the murderer is at large. This is the second bad case, Parr, and I'll tell you candidly that it is my intention to act on the advice which this newspaper gives."

He tapped the cutting suggestively.

"On the previous occasion you allowed Mr. Yale to get away with all the kudos for the capture of the murderer. You have seen Mr. Yale, I presume?"

The detective nodded.

"And what does he say?"

Mr. Parr shifted uneasily on his feet.

"He told me a lot of nonsense about a dark man with toothache."

"How did he get that?" asked the Commissioner quickly.

"From the shell of the cartridge he found on the ground," said the detective. "I don't take any notice of this psychometrical stuff—"

The Commissioner leant back in his chair and sighed.

"I don't think you take notice of any stuff that is serviceable. Parr," he said, "and don't sneer at Yale. That man has unusual and peculiar gifts. The fact that you don't understand them does not make them any less peculiar."

"Do you mean to say, sir," said Parr, stirred into protest, "that a man can take a cartridge in his hand and tell you from that the appearance of the person who last handled it and what he was thinking about? Why, it is absurd!"

"Nothing is absurd," said the Commissioner quietly. "The science of psychometry has been practised for years. Some people, unusually sensitive to impression, are able to tell the most remarkable things, and Yale is one of these."

"He was there when the murder was committed," replied Parr. "He was with Mr. Beardmore's son, not a hundred yards away, and yet he did not catch the murderer."

The Commissioner nodded. "Neither have you," he said. "Twelve months ago you told me of your scheme for trapping the Crimson Circle, and I agreed. We've both expected a little too much for your plan, I think. You must try something else. I hate to say it, but there it is."

Parr did not answer for a time, and then to the Commissioner's surprise, he pulled up a chair to the desk and sat down uninvited.

"Colonel," he said, "I'm going to tell you something," and he was so earnest, so unlike his usual self, that the Commissioner could only look at him in amazement.

"The Crimson Circle gang is easy to get. I can find every one of them, and will find them if you will give me time. But it is the hub of the wheel that I'm after. If I can get the hub the spokes don't count. But you've got to give me a little more authority that I have at present."

"A little more authority?" said the dumbfounded Commissioner. "What the devil do you mean?"

"I'll explain," said the bovine Mr. Parr, and he explained to such purpose that he left the Commissioner a very silent and a very thoughtful man.

After he left head-quarters, Mr. Parr's first call was at an office in the centre of the city.

On the third floor, in a tiny suite, which was distinguished only by the name of the occupant, Mr. Derrick Yale was waiting for him, and a greater contrast between the two men could not be imagined.

Yale, the overstrung, nervous, and sensitive dreamer; Parr, solid and beefy, seemingly incapable of an independent thought.

"How did your interview go on, Parr?"

"Not very well," said Parr, ruefully. "I think the Commissioner's got one against me. Have you discovered anything?"

"I've discovered your man with the tooth-ache," was the astonishing reply. "His name is Sibly; he is a seafaring man, and was seen in the vicinity of the house the following day. Yesterday," he picked up a telegram, "he was arrested for drunken and' disorderly conduct, and in his possession was found an automatic pistol, which I should imagine was the weapon with which the crime was committed. You remember that the bullet which was extracted from poor Beardmore, was obviously fired from an automatic."

Parr gaped at him in amazement.

"How did you find this out?"

And Derrick Yale laughed softly. "You haven't a great deal of faith in my deductions," he said with a glint of humour in his eyes. "But when I felt that cartridge I was as certain that I could see the man as I am certain I can see you. I sent one of my own staff down to make enquiries, with this result." He picked up the telegram.

Mr. Parr stood, a heavy frown disfiguring what little claim to beauty he might have.

"So they've caught him," he said softly. "Now I wonder if he wrote this?"

He took out a pocket-book, and Derrick Yale saw him extract a scrap of paper which had evidently been burnt, for the edges were black.

Yale took the scrap from his hand.

"Where did you find this?" he asked.

"I raked it out of the ashpan at Beardmore's place yesterday," he said.

The writing was in a large scrawling hand, and the scrap ran:

You alone me alone Block B Graft

"Me alone.. you alone,'" read Yale. "'Block B.. Graft'?" He shook his head. "It is Greek to me."

He balanced the letter upon the palm of his hand and shook his head.

"I can't even feel an impression," he said. "Fire destroys the aura."

Parr carefully put away the scrap into his case and replaced it in his pocket.

"There is another thing I'd like to tell you," he said. "Somebody was in the wood who wore pointed shoes and smoked cigars. I found the cigar ashes in a little hollow, and his footprint was on the flower-beds."

"Near the house?" asked Derrick Yale, startled,

The solid man nodded.

"My own theory is," he went on, "that somebody wanted to warn Beardmore, wrote this letter and brought it to the house after dark. It must have been received by the old man, because he burnt it. I found the ashes in the place where the servants dump their cinders."

There was a gentle tap at the door.

"Jack Beardmore," said Yale under his breath.

Jack Beardmore showed signs of the distressing period through which he had passed. He nodded to Parr and came toward Yale with outstretched hand.

"No news, I suppose?" he asked, and turning to the other: "You were at the house yesterday, Mr. Parr. Did you find anything?"

"Nothing worth speaking about," said Parr.

"I've just been to see Froyant, he is in town," said Jack. "It wasn't a very successful visit, for he is in a pitiable state of nerves." He did not explain that the unsatisfactory part of his call was that he had not seen Thalia Drummond, and only one of the men guessed the reason of his disappointment.

Derrick Yale told him of the arrest which had been made.

"I don't want you to build any hopes on this," he said, "even if he is the man who tired the shot, he is certain to be no more than the agent. We shall probably hear the same story as we heard before, that he was in low water and that the chief of the Crimson Circle induced him to commit the act. We are as far from the real solution as ever we have been."

They strolled out of the office together, into the clean autumn sunlight.

Jack, who had an engagement with a lawyer who was settling his father's estate, accompanied the two men, who were on their way to catch a train for the town where the suspected murderer was detained. They were passing through one of the busiest streets when Jack uttered an exclamation. On the opposite side of the road was a big pawnbroker's, and a girl was coming from the side entrance devoted to the service of those who needed temporary loans.

"Well, I'm blessed!" It was Parr's unemotional voice. "I haven't seen her for two years."

Jack turned on him open-eyed. "Haven't seen her for two years," he said slowly. "Are you referring to that lady?"

Parr nodded.

"I'm referring to Thalia Drummond," he said calmly, "who is a crook and a companion of crooks!"

CHAPTER VII

THE STOLEN IDOL

JACK heard him and was stunned. He stood motionless and speechless, as the girl, as though unconscious of the scrutiny, hailed a taxi-cab and was driven away.

"Now what the dickens was she doing there?" said Parr.

"A crook and a companion of crooks," repeated Jack mechanically. "Good God! Where are you going?" he asked quickly, as the inspector took a step into the roadway.

"I intend discovering what she has been doing in the pawnbroker's," said the stolid Parr.

"She may have gone there because she was short of money. It is no crime to be short of money."

Jack realised the feebleness of his defence even as he spoke. Thalia Drummond a thief! It was incredible, impossible! And yet he followed unresistingly the detective as he crossed the road; followed him down the dark passage to the loaning department, and was present in the manager's room when an assistant brought in the article which the girl had pledged. It was a small golden figure of Buddha.

"I thought it queer," said the manager, when Parr had made himself known. "She only wanted ten pounds and it is worth a hundred if it's worth a penny."

"What explanation did she give?" asked Derrick Yale, who had been a silent listener.

"She said she was short of money and that her father had a number of these curios, but wanted to pledge them at a price which would allow him to redeem them."

"Did she leave her address? What name did she give?"

"Thalia Drummond," said the assistant, "of 29, Park Gate."

Derrick Yale uttered an exclamation. "Why, that's Froyant's address, isn't it?"

Too well Jack knew it was the address of the miserly Harvey Froyant, and he remembered with a sinking of heart that Froyant made a hobby of collecting these eastern antiquities. The inspector gave a receipt for the idol and slipped it into his pocket.

"We'll go along and see Mr. Froyant," he said, and Jack interposed desperately: "For heaven's sake, don't let us get this girl into trouble," he pleaded. "It may have been some sudden temptation—I will make things right, if money can settle the affair."

Derrick Yale was eyeing the young man with a grave, understanding look.

"You know Miss Drummond?"

Jack nodded. He was too miserable to speak; he felt an absurd desire to run away and hide himself.

"It can't be done," said Inspector Parr definitely. He was the conventional police officer now. "I'm going along to Froyant's to discover whether this article was pledged with his approval."

"Then you'll go by yourself," said Jack wrathfully.

He could not contemplate being a witness of the girl's humiliation. It was monstrous. It was beastly of Parr, he said to Yale when they were alone.

"The girl would not commit so mean a theft, the stupid, blundering fool! I wish to heaven I had never called his attention to her."

"It was he who saw her first," said Yale, and dropped his hand upon the young man's shoulder. "Jack, you're a little unstrung, I think. Why are you so interested in Miss Drummond? Of course," he said suddenly, "you must have seen a lot of her when you were at home. Froyant's estate joins yours, doesn't it?"

Jack nodded.

"If he would give as much attention to the running down of the Crimson Circle as he gives to the hounding of that poor girl," he said bitterly, "my poor father would be alive to-day."

Derrick Yale did his best to soothe him. He took him back to his office and tried to bring his thoughts to a more pleasant channel. They had been there a quarter of an hour when the telephone bell rang. It was Parr who spoke.

"Well?" asked Yale.

"I've arrested Thalia Drummond, and I am charging her in the morning," was the laconic message.

Yale put down the receiver gently and turned to the young man,

"She's arrested?" Jack guessed before he spoke.

Yale nodded.

Jack Beardmore's face was very white.

"You see, Jack," said Yale gently, "you have probably been as much deceived as Froyant. The girl is a thief."

"If she were a thief and murderess," said Jack doggedly, "I love her."

CHAPTER VIII

THE CHARGE

MR. PARR'S interview with Harvey Froyant was a short one. At the sight of the detective, that thin man blanched. He knew him by sight and had met him in connection with the Beardmore tragedy.

"Well, well," he asked tremulously. "What is wrong? Have these infernal people started a new campaign?"

"Nothing so bad as that, sir," said Parr. "I came to ask you a few questions. How long have you had Thalia Drummond in your house?"

"She has been my secretary for three months," said Froyant suspiciously. "Why?"

"What wages do you pay her?" asked Parr.

Mr. Froyant mentioned a sum grossly inadequate, and even he was apologetic for its inefficiency.

"I give her her food, you know, and she has evenings off," he said, feeling that the starvation wage must be justified.

"Has she been short of money lately?"

Mr. Froyant stared at him.

"Why—yes. She asked me if I could advance her five pounds yesterday," he said. "She said she had a call upon her purse which she could not meet. Of course, I didn't advance the money. I do not approve of advancing money for work which is not performed," said Froyant virtuously. "It tends to pauperise—"

"You have a large number of antiques, I understand, Mr. Froyant, some of them very valuable. Have you missed any lately?"

Froyant jumped to his feet. The very hint that he might have been robbed was sufficient to set his mind in a panic. Without a word he rushed from the room. He was gone three minutes and when he came back his eyes were almost bulging from his head.

"My Buddha!" he gasped. "It is worth a hundred pounds. It was there this morning—"

"Send for Miss Drummond," said the detective briefly.

Thalia came, a cool, self-possessed girl, who stood by her employer's desk, her hands clasped behind her, scarcely looking at the detective.

The interview was short, and for Mr. Froyant, painful. Upon the girl it had no apparent effect whatever. And yet she must have known, from the steely glare in Froyant's eyes, that her theft had been detected. For a little time the man found a difficulty in framing a coherent sentence.

"You—you have stolen something of mine," he blurted out. His voice was almost a squeak. The accusing hand trembled in the intensity of his emotion. "You—you are a thief!"

"I asked you for the money," said the girl coolly. "If you hadn't been such a wicked old skinflint, you'd have let me have it."

"You—you—" spluttered Froyant, and then with a gasp—"I charge her, inspector. I charge her with theft. You shall go to prison for this. Mark my words, young woman. Wait—wait," he raised his hand. "I will see if anything else is missing."

"You can save yourself the trouble," said the girl, as he was leaving the room. "The Buddha was the only thing I took, and it was an ugly little beast anyway."

"Give me your keys," stormed the enraged man. "To think that I've allowed you to open my business letters!"

"I've opened one which will not be pleasant for you, Mr. Froyant," she said quietly, and then he saw what she was holding in her hand.

She passed the envelope across to him, and with staring eyes he saw the Crimson Circle, but the words written within the hoop were blurred and indistinct. He dropped the card and collapsed into a chair.

CHAPTER IX

THALIA IN THE POLICE COURT

THE magistrate was a kind-hearted man and seemed uncomfortable. He looked from the unemotional Mr. Parr who stood on the witness-stand, to the girl in the steel pen, and she was almost as cool and as self-controlled as the police witness. Her face was one which would have attracted attention in any circumstances, but in the drab setting of the police court, her beauty was emphasised and enhanced.

The magistrate glanced down at the charge-sheet before him. Her age was described as twenty-one, her occupation as secretary.

The man of law, who had had many shocks in his lifetime, and had steeled himself to the most unusual and improbable happenings, could only shake his head in despair. "Is anything known against this woman?" he asked, and felt it was absurd even to refer to the slim, girlish prisoner as a "woman."

"She has been under observation for some time, your worship," was the reply, "but she has not been in the hands of the police before."

The magistrate looked over his glasses at the girl.

"I cannot understand how you got yourself into this terrible position," he said. "A girl who has evidently had the education of a lady, you have been charged with a theft of a few pounds, for although the article you stole was worth a large sum, that was all that your dishonesty realised. Your act was probably due to some great temptation. I suppose the need for the money was very urgent; yet that does not excuse your act. I shall bind you over to come up for judgment when called upon, treating you as a first offender, and I do most earnestly appeal to you to live honestly and avoid a repetition of this unpleasant experience." The girl bowed slightly and left the box for the police office, and the next case was called.

Harvey Froyant rose at the same time and made his way out of the court. He was a rich man to whom money represented the goal and object of life. He was the type of man who counted the contents of his pocket every night before he went to bed, and he would have had his own mother arrested in similar circumstances. Thalia Drummond's offence was made more hideous in his eyes because her last act of service had been to hand to him the warning of the Crimson Circle, from the shock of which he had not yet recovered. He was a large, thin man with a permanent stoop. His attitude towards the world was one of acute suspicion; for the moment it was one of resentment, for he held the strongest views on the sacredness of property.

To Parr, who followed him out of the court, he expressed his disappointment that the girl had not been sent to prison.

"A woman like that is a danger to society," he complained in his high-pitched, peevish voice. "How do I know that she isn't in league with these blackguards who are threatening me? Pony thousand they ask for! Forty thousand!" He wailed the last words. "It is your duty to see that I come to no harm! Understand that—it is your duty!"

"I heard you!" said Inspector Parr wearily. "And as to the girl, I don't suppose she ever heard of the Crimson Circle. She's very young."

"Young!" snarled the lean man. "That's the time to punish them, isn't it? Catch them young and punish them young, and you may turn them into respectable citizens!"

"I dare say you're right," agreed the stout Mr. Parr with a sigh, and then inconsequently, "Children are a great responsibility."

Froyant muttered something under his breath, and without so much as a nod of farewell, walked rapidly through the court, into the motor-car which was waiting for him at the entrance to the court-house.

The inspector watched him depart with a slow smile, and, looking round, caught the eye of a young man who was waiting by the clerk's door.

"Good morning, Mr. Beardmore," he said. "Are you waiting to see the young lady?"

"Yes. How long will they keep her?" asked Jack nervously.

Mr. Parr gazed at him with expressionless eyes, and sniffed.

"If you don't mind my saying so, Mr. Beardmore," he said quietly, "you are probably taking a greater interest in Miss Drummond than is good for you."

"What do you mean?" asked Jack quietly. "The whole thing was a plot. That beast Froyant—"

The inspector shook his head. "Miss Drummond admitted that she took the statuette," he said, "and, besides, we saw her coming out of Isaacs. There isn't any doubt about it."

"She only made the admission for some reason best known to herself," said Jack violently. "Do you think a girl like that would steal? Why should she? I would have given her anything she wanted "—he checked himself suddenly. "There is something behind this," he went on more quietly, "something which I do not understand, and probably you do not understand either, inspector,"

The door opened at that moment and the girl came out. She stopped at the sight of Jack and a faint flush crept into her pale face.

"Were you in court?" she asked quickly. He nodded, and she shook her head. "You shouldn't have come," she said almost vehemently. "How did you know? Who told you?" She seemed oblivious to the presence of the inspector, but for the first time since her arrest she showed some sign of her pent emotion. The colour came and went, and her voice shook a little as she continued: "I am sorry you knew anything about it, Mr. Beardmore, and am desperately sorry you came," she said.

"But it isn't true," he interrupted. "You can tell me that, Thalia? It was a plot, wasn't it? A plot intended to ruin you?" His voice was almost pleading, but she shook her head.

"There was no plot," she said quietly, "I stole from Mr. Froyant."

"But why, why?" he asked despairingly. "Why did you—"

"I am afraid I can't tell you why," she said with the ghost of a smile on her lips, "except that I needed the money, and that is good and sufficient reason, isn't it?"

"I'll never believe it." Jack's face was set and his grey eyes regarded her steadily. "You are not the kind who would indulge in petty pilfering."

She looked at him for a long time, and then turned her eyes to the inspector.

"You may be able to undeceive Mr. Beardmore," she said. "I am afraid I cannot."

"Where are you going?" he asked as, with a little nod, she was passing on.

"I am going home," she replied. "Please don't come with me, Mr. Beardmore."

"But you have no home."

"I have a lodging," she said with a hint of impatience.

"Then I am going with you," he said doggedly. She did not make any remonstrance, and they passed from the court together into the busy street. No word was spoken until they reached the entrance of a tube station.

"Now I must go home," she said more gently than before.

"But what are you going to do?" he demanded. "How are you going to get your living with this terrible charge against you?"

"Is it so terrible?" she asked coolly. She was walking into the station entrance when he took her arm and swung her round with almost savage violence.

"Now listen to me, Thalia," he said between his teeth. "I love you and I want to marry you. I haven't told you that before, but you've guessed it. I am not going to allow you to go out of my life. Do you understand that? I do not believe that you are a thief and—"

Very gently she disengaged his grip.

"Mr. Beardmore," she said in a low voice, "you are just being quixotic and foolish! You have told me what you will not allow, and I tell you that I am not going to allow you to ruin your life through your infatuation for a convicted thief. You know nothing of me except that I am a seemingly nice girl whom you met by accident in the country, and it is my duty to be your mother and your maiden aunt." There was a glint of amusement in her eye as she took his offered hand. "Some day perhaps we shall meet again, and by that time the glamour of romance will have worn off. Good-bye."

She had disappeared into the booking hall before he could find his voice.

CHAPTER X

THE SUMMONS OF THE CRIMSON CIRCLE

THALIA DRUMMOND went back to the lodging she had occupied before she had entered Mr. Harvey Froyant's service as resident secretary, and apparently the story of her ill-deeds had preceded her, for the stout landlady gave her a chilly welcome, and had she not continued to pay the rent of her one room during the time she was working for Froyant, it was probable that she would not have been admitted.

It was a small room, neatly if plainly furnished, and oblivious to the landlady's glum face and cold reception, she went to her apartment and locked the door behind her. She had spent a very unpleasant week, for she had been remanded in custody, and her very clothes seemed to exhale the musty odour of Holloway Gaol. Holloway, however, had an advantage which No. 14, Lexington Street, did not possess. It had an admirable system of bathrooms, for which the girl was truly grateful as she began to change.

She had plenty to occupy her mind. Harvey Froyant...Jack Beardmore...she frowned as though at a distasteful thought, and tried to dismiss him from her mind. It was a relief to go back to Froyant. She almost hated him. She certainly despised him. The time she had spent in his house had been the most wretched period in her life. She had taken her meals with the servants and had been conscious that every scrap of food she ate had been measured and weighed and duly apportioned by a man whose cheque for seven figures would have been honoured. "At least, he didn't make love to you, my dear," she said to herself, and smiled. Somehow she couldn't imagine Harvey Froyant making love to anybody. She recalled the days she had followed him about his big house with a note-book in her hand, whilst he searched for evidence of his servants' neglect, drawing his fingers along the polished shelves in the library in a vain search for dust, turning up carpet corners, examining silver, or else counting, as he did regularly every week, the contents of his still-room, He measured the wine at table and counted the empty bottles, even the corks. It was his boast that in his big garden he could tell the absence of a flower. These he sent to market regularly, with the vegetables he grew and the peaches which ripened on the wall, and woe betide the unlucky gardener who had poached so much as a ripe apple from the orchard, for Harvey had an uncanny instinct which led him to the rifled tree.

She smiled a little wryly at the recollection, and, having completed her change of costume, she went out, locking the door behind her. Her landlady watched her pass down the street, and nodded ominously.

"Your lodger's come back," said a neighbour.

"Yes, she's come back," said the woman grimly. "A nice lady she is—I don't think! It is the first time I've ever had a crook in my house, and it'll be the last. I am giving her notice to-night."

Unconscious of the criticism, Thalia boarded a bus which took her into the city. She got down in Fleet Street, went into the large office of a popular newspaper. At the desk she took an advertisement form, looked at the white sheet for a moment thoughtfully, then wrote:

SECRETARY.—Young lady from the Colonies requires post as Secretary. Resident-Secretary preferred. Small wages required. Shorthand and Typewriting.

She left a space for the box number, handed the advertisement across the counter, and paid the fee.

She was back again in Lexington Street in time for tea, a meal which was brought up to her on a battered tray by her landlady.

"Look here. Miss Drummond," said that worthy person,

"I've got a few words to say to you."

"Say them," said the girl carelessly.

"I shall want your room after next week."

Thalia turned slowly. "Does that mean I've got to get out?"

"That's what it means. I can't have people like you staying in a respectable house. I'm surprised at you, a young lady as I always thought you were."

"Continue to think so," said Thalia coolly. "I'm both young and ladylike."

But the stout landlady was not to be checked in her well-rehearsed indictment.

"A nice lady you are," she said, "giving my house a bad name. You've been in prison for a week. Perhaps you don't think I know, but I read the newspapers."

"I'm sure you do," said the girl quietly. "That will do, Mrs. Boled. I leave your house next week."

"And I should like to say—" began the woman.

"Say it on the mat," said Thalia, and closed the door in the choleric lady's face.

As it was now growing dark, she lit a kerosene lamp and occupied the evening by manicuring her nails, an operation which was interrupted by the arrival of the nine o'clock post. She heard the rat-tat at the door and the heavy feet of her landlady on the stairs.

"A letter for you," called the woman. Thalia unlocked the door and took the envelope from the landlady's hand. "You had better tell your friends that you're going to get a new address," said the woman, loath to leave her quarrel half-finished.

"I haven't told my friends yet that I live in such a horrible place," said Thalia sweetly, and locked the door before the woman could think of a suitable reply.

She smiled as she carried the envelope to the light. It was addressed in printed characters. She turned it over, looking at the postmark before she opened it, and extracted a thick white card. At the first glance of the message her face changed its expression.

The card was a square one, and in the centre was a large crimson circle. Within the circle was written in the same printed characters:

"We have need of you. Enter the car which you will find waiting at the corner of Steyne Square at ten o'clock to-morrow night."

She put the card down on the table and stared at it.

The Crimson Circle had need of her! She had expected the summons, but it had come earlier than she had anticipated.

CHAPTER XI

THE CONFESSION

AT three minutes to ten the following night, a closed car drove slowly into Steyne Square and came to a halt at the corner of Clarges Street. A few minutes later Thalia Drummond walked into the square from the other end. She wore a long black cloak, and the little hat upon her head was held in its position by a thick veil knotted under her chin.

Without a second's hesitation she opened the door of the car and stepped in. It was in complete darkness, but she could see the figure of the driver indistinctly. He did not turn his head, nor did he attempt to start the car, although she felt the vibration of the engines beneath her feet.

"You were charged at the Marylebone Police Court yesterday morning with theft," said the driver without preamble. "Yesterday afternoon you inserted an advertisement, describing yourself as a newly-arrived colonial, your intention being to find another situation, where you could continue your career of petty pilfering."

"This is very interesting," said Thalia without a tremor of voice, "but you did not bring me here to give me my past history. When I had your letter I guessed that you thought I would be a very useful assistant. But there is one question I want to ask you."

"If I wish to reply I shall," was the uncompromising answer.

"I realise that," said Thalia, with a faint smile in the darkness. "Suppose I had communicated with the police and I had come here attended by Mr. Parr and the clever Mr. Derrick Yale?"

"You would have been lying on the pavement dead by now," was the calm announcement. "Miss Drummond, I am going to put easy money in your way and find you a very excellent job. I do not even mind if you indulge in your eccentricity in your spare time, but your principal task will be to serve me. You understand?"

She nodded, and then realising he could not see her, she said: "Yes."

"You will be paid well for everything you do; I shall always be on hand to help you—or to punish you if you attempt to betray me," he added. "Do you understand?"

"Perfectly," she replied,

"Your job will be a very simple one," went on the unknown driver. "You will present yourself at Brabazon's Bank to-morrow. Brabazon is in need of a secretary."

"But will he employ me?" she interrupted. "Must I go in another name?"

"Go in your own name," said the man impatiently. "Don't interrupt. I will pay you two hundred pounds for your services. Here is the money." He thrust two notes over his shoulder and she took them.

Her hand accidentally touched his shoulder, and she felt something hard beneath his fleecy coat.

"A bullet-proof waistcoat," she noted mentally, and then aloud: "What am I to say to Mr. Brabazon about my earlier experience?"

"It will be unnecessary to say anything, or do anything. You will receive your instructions from time to time. That is all," he added shortly.

A few minutes later Thalia Drummond sat in the corner of the taxi-cab which was taking her back to Lexington Street. Behind her, at intervals, came another taxi-cab which slowed when hers did, but never overtook her, not even when she descended at the comer of the street where her lodgings were situated. And when she turned the key of her street door, Inspector Parr was only a dozen paces from her. If she knew that she was being shadowed, she made no sign.

Parr only waited for a few minutes, watching the house from the opposite side of the roadway, and then; as her light appeared in the upper window, he turned and walked thoughtfully back to the cab which had brought him so far eastward.

He had opened the door of the cab and was stepping in, when somebody passed him on the side-walk; somebody who was walking briskly with his collar turned up, but Inspector Parr knew him.

'Flush', he called sharply, and the man turned round on his heel.

He was a little dark, thin-faced, lithe man, at the sight of the Inspector his jaw dropped.

"Why—why, Mr. Parr," he said, with ill-affected geniality, "whoever thought of seeing you in this part of the world?"

"I want a little talk with you. Flush. Will you walk along with me?"

It was an ominous invitation, which Mr. 'Flush' had heard before.

"You haven't got anything against me, Mr. Parr?" he said loudly.

"Nothing," admitted Parr. "Besides, you're going straight now. I seem to remember you telling me that day you came out of prison."

"That's right," said 'Flush' Barnet, heaving a sigh of relief. "Going straight, working for my living, and engaged to be married."

"You don't tell me?" said the stout Mr. Parr with simulated astonishment. "And is it Bella or Milly?"

"It is Milly," said 'Flush', inwardly cursing the excellent memory of the police inspector. "She's going straight, too. She's got a job at one of the shops."

"At Brabazon's Bank, to be exact," said the inspector, and then turned as though some thought had arrested him. "I wonder," he muttered, "I wonder if that is it?"

"She's a perfect young lady, is Milly," Mr. 'Flush' hastened to explain. "Honest as the day, wouldn't swipe a clock, not if her life depended on it. I don't want you to think she is bad, Mr. Parr, because she's not. We're both living what I might term an honest life."

Parr's placid face wrinkled in a smile. "That's grand news you're telling me, Flush. Where is Milly to be found in these days?"

"She's living in diggings on the other side of the river," said 'Flush' reluctantly. "You're not going to rake up old scandals, are you, Mr. Parr?"

"Heaven forbid," said Inspector Parr piously. "No, I'd like to have a talk with her. Perhaps—" he hesitated, "anyway, it can wait. It was rather providential meeting you, 'Flush'."

But 'Flush' did not share that view, even though he expressed a faint acquiescence.

"So that's it," said Inspector Parr to himself, but he did not express the nature of his suspicions, even when he met Derrick Yale at his club half-an-hour later. And it was a further curious fact, that though they touched every aspect of the Crimson Circle mystery in the long conversation which followed, never once did Mr. Parr mention Thalia Drummond's interview, which, if he had not seen, he had at least guessed.

The two men left early the next morning for the little country town where one Ambrose Sibly, described as an able-seaman, was held on a charge of murder. At his own earnest request, Jack Beardmore was allowed to accompany them, though he was not present at the interview between the two detectives and the sullen man who had slain his father.

A brawny, unshaven fellow, half Scottish, half Swede, Sibly proved to be. He could neither read nor write, and had been in the hands of the police before. This much Parr had discovered from a reference of his fingerprints.

At first he was not inclined to commit himself, and it was rather Derrick Yale's skilful cross-examination, than Inspector Parr's efforts, which produced the confession.

"Yes, I did it all right," he said at last. They were seated in the cell with an official shorthand-writer taking a note of his statement.

"You've got me proper, but you wouldn't have got me if I hadn't been drunk. And whilst I'm confessing, I might as well own up that I killed Harry Hobbs. He was a shipmate of mine on the Oritianga in 1912—they can only hang me once. Killed him and chucked his body overboard, I did, over the question of a woman that we met at Newport News, which is in America. I'll tell you how this happened, gentlemen. I lost my ship about a month ago, and was stranded at the Sailors' Home at Wapping. I got chucked out of there for being drunk, and on top of that I was locked up and got seven days' imprisonment. If the old fool had only given me a month I shouldn't have been here. One night after I came out of prison I was walking through the East End, down on my luck and starving for a drink, and feeling properly miserable. To make it worse, I had the toothache—" Parr met Derrick Yale's eyes, and Derrick smiled faintly.

"I was loafing along the edge of the pavement looking for cigarette ends, and thinking of nothing except where I could get a bit of food and a night's lodging. It was beginning to rain, too, and it looked as though I was going to have another night on the streets, when I heard a voice say, almost in my ear, 'Jump in.' I looked round. A motor-car was standing by the side of the roadway. I couldn't believe my ears. Presently the man in the car said 'Jump in. It's you I mean!' and he mentioned my name. We drove along for a while without his saying anything, and I noticed that he kept clear of all the streets where the big lights were.

"After a bit he stopped the car, and began to tell me who I was. I can assure you I was surprised. He knew the whole of my history. He even knew about Harry Hobbs—I was tried for that killing and acquitted—and then he asked me if I'd like to earn a hundred pounds. I told him I would, and he said there was an old gentleman in the country who had done him a lot of harm, and he wanted him 'outed.' I didn't want to take the job on for some time, but he gave me such a lot of talk about how he could get me hung for Hobbs's murder, and how it was safe, and he'd give me a bicycle to get away on, and at last I agreed.

"He picked me up by arrangement a week later in Steyne Square. Then he gave me all the final particulars. I got down to Beardmore's place soon after it was dark, and hid in the wood. He told me Mr. Beardmore generally walked through the wood every morning, and that I was to make myself comfortable for the night. I hadn't been in the wood an hour when I had a fright. I heard somebody moving. I think it must have been a game-keeper. He was a big fellow, and I only just got a glimpse of him.

"And I think that's about all, gentlemen, except that the next morning the old fellow came in the wood and I shot him. I don't remember much about it, for I was drunk at the time, having taken a bottle of whisky into the wood with me. But I was sober enough to get on to the bicycle, and I rode off. And I should have got away altogether, if it hadn't been for the booze."

"And that is all?" asked Parr, when the confession had been read over and the man had affixed a rough cross.

"That's all, guv'nor," said the sailor.

"And you don't know who it was who employed you?"

"Not the faintest idea," said the other cheerfully. "There's one thing about him, though, I could tell you," he said after a pause. "He kept using a word that I've never heard before. I'm not highly educated, but I've noticed that some men have favourite words. We had an old skipper who always used the word 'morbid'."

"What was the word?" asked Parr.

The man scratched his head. "I'll remember it and let you know," he said, and they left him to his meditations, which were few, and probably not unpleasant.

Four hours after, the jailor took Ambrose Sibly some food. He was lying on his bed, and the jailor shook him by the shoulder.

"Wake up," he said, but Ambrose Sibly never woke again.

He was stone dead. And in the tin dipper, half-filled with water, which stood by his bed, and with which he had slaked his thirst, they found sufficient hydrocyanic acid to kill fifty men.

But it was not the poison which interested Inspector Parr so much as the little circle of crimson paper which was found floating on the top of the water.

CHAPTER XII

THE POINTED BOOTS

MR. FELIX MARL sat behind the locked door of his bedroom, and he was engaged in a task which had the elements of unpleasant familiarity.

Twenty-five years before, when he was an inmate of the big French prison at Toulouse, he had worked in a bootmaker's shop, and the handling of boots was an everyday experience. It is true his business had been to repair, and not to destroy. To-day, with a razor-sharp knife, he was cutting to shreds a pair of pointed patent leather shoes which he had only worn three times. Strip by strip he cut the leather, which he then placed on the fire.

Some men live intensely and suffer intensely, Mr. Felix Marl was one of those who could crowd into a day the terrors of an aeon. In some manner a newspaper had got hold of the story of the footprint in Beardmore's ground, and a new fear had been added to the many which confused and paralysed this big man. He was sitting in his shirt sleeves, the perspiration rolling down his face, for the fire was a big one and the room was super-heated.

Presently the last shred was thrown into the fire and he sat watching it grill and flame before he put away the knife, washed his hands and opened the windows to let out the acrid odour of burning leather.

It would have been better, he thought, if he had carried out his first resolution, and he cursed himself for the cowardice which had induced him to substitute his revolver for a fountain pen. But he was safe. Nobody had seen him leave the grounds.

With such men as he, blind panic and unreasoning confidence succeed one another, almost as a natural reaction. By the time he had descended his stairs to his little library he had almost forgotten that he was in any danger.

In the fading light of day he had written a conciliatory, even a grovelling letter, and had, as he believed, delivered it safely. Would it be found? He had another moment of panic.

"Pshaw!" said Mr. Marl, and dismissed that dangerous possibility.

His servant brought him a tea-tray and arranged it on a small table by the side of his desk, where the big man sat. "Will you see that gentleman now, sir?"

"Eh?" said Mr. Marl, turning round. "Which gentleman?"

"I told you there was a man who wanted to see you."

Marl remembered that his boot-destroying operation had been interrupted by a knock. "Who is he?" he asked. "I put his card on the table, sir."

"Didn't you tell him that I was engaged?"

"Yes, but he said he'd wait until you came down." The man handed him the card, and Mr. Marl reading it, jumped and turned a sickly yellow.

"Inspector Parr," he said unsteadily. "What does he want with me?"

His shaking hand fingered his mouth.

"Show him in," he said with an effort.

He had not met Inspector Parr either professionally or socially, and his first glance at the little man reassured him. There was nothing particularly menacing in the appearance of the red-faced detective.

"Sit down, inspector. I'm sorry I was busy when you came," said Mr. Marl. When he was agitated his voice was almost bird-like in its thinness.

Parr sat down on the edge of the nearest chair, balancing his Derby hat on his knee.

"I thought I'd wait until you came down, Mr. Marl. I wanted to see you about this Beardmore murder."

Mr. Marl said nothing. With an effort he kept his trembling lips from quivering, and assumed, as he believed, an air of polite interest.

"You knew Mr. Beardmore very well?"

"Not very well," said Marl. "I certainly have had business dealings with him."

"Have you met him before?"

Marl hesitated. He was the kind of man to whom a lie came most readily, and his natural habit of mind was to state the exact opposite of the truth.

"No," he admitted. "I had seen him years ago, but that was before he had grown a beard."

"Where was Mr. Beardmore when you were coming into the house?" asked Parr.

"He was standing on the terrace," replied Marl with unnecessary loudness.

"And you saw him?"

Marl nodded.

"They tell me, Mr. Marl," Parr went on, looking down at his hat, "that for some reason or other you were startled—Mr. Jack Beardmore says that he thought you were momentarily terrified. What was the cause of that?"

Mr. Marl shrugged his shoulders and forced a smile.

"I think I explained it was a little heart attack. I am subject to them," he said.

Pan-had turned his hat so that he was looking into the interior, and he did not raise his eyes when he asked: "It was not the sight of Mr. Beardmore?"

"Of course not," said the other vigorously. "Why should I be scared of Mr. Beardmore? I've had a lot of correspondence with him, and know him almost as well— "

"But you hadn't met him for years?"

"I hadn't seen him for years," corrected Marl irritably.

"And the cause of your agitation was just a heart attack, Mr. Marl?" asked the inspector.

For the first time his eyes rose and fixed themselves upon the other's.

"Absolutely." Marl's voice did not lack heartiness. "I had forgotten all about my little seizure until you reminded me."

"There is another point I wanted cleared up," said the detective. His attention had gone back to his fascinating hat, which he was turning over and over mechanically until it had the appearance of a revolving butter-churn. "When you came to Mr. Beardmore's house you were wearing pointed patent shoes."

Marl frowned.

"Was I? I've forgotten."

"Did you take any walk into the grounds, except the walk you had from the railway station?"

"No."

"You didn't walk around the house to admire the—er—architecture?"

"No, I did not. I was only in the house a few minutes, and then I drove away."

Mr. Parr raised his eyes to the ceiling.

"Would it be asking you too much," he demanded apologetically, "if I requested you to show me the patent shoes you wore that day?"

"Certainly," said Marl, rising with alacrity.

He was out of the room a few minutes, and came back with a pair of long pointed patent boots.

The detective took them in his hand and looked earnestly at the sole.

"Yes," he said. "Of course, these are not the boots you were wearing, because—" he rubbed the soles gently with his hand, "there is dust on them, and the ground has been wet for the last week."

Marl's heart nearly stopped beating.

"Those are the boots I wore," he said defiantly. "What you call 'dust' is really dried mud."

Parr looked at his dusty fingers and shook his head.

"I think there must be some mistake, Mr. Marl," he said gently. "This is chalk dust." He put the boots down and rose. "However, it isn't very important," he said. He stood so long, looking down at the carpet, that Mr. Marl, in spite of his fear, became impatient.

"Is there anything more I can do for you, officer?" he asked.

"Yes," said Parr. "I want you to give me the name and address of your tailor. Perhaps you would write it down for me."

"My tailor?" Mr. Marl glared at the visitor. "What the dickens do you want of my tailor?" And then, with a laugh, "Well, you are a curious man, inspector; but I'll do it with pleasure."

He went to his secretaire, pulled out a sheet of paper, wrote down a name and address and, blotting it, handed it to the detective.

"Thank you, sir." Parr did not even look at the address, but put the paper into his pocket.

"I'm sorry to bother you, but you will realise that everybody who was present at the house within twenty-four hours of Mr. Beardmore's death must necessarily be interrogated. The Crimson Circle—"

"The Crimson Circle!" gasped Mr. Marl, and the detective looked at him straightly.

"Didn't you know that the Crimson Circle were responsible for this murder?"

To do him justice, Mr. Felix Marl knew nothing of the kind. He had seen a brief report that James Beardmore had been found shot but the association of the murder with the Crimson Circle had not been disclosed except by the Monitor, a newspaper which Mr. Marl never read.

He dropped into a chair, quaking. "The Crimson Circle," he muttered. "Good God—I never thought—" he checked himself.

"What didn't you think?" asked Parr gently.

"The Crimson Circle," murmured the big man again. "I thought it was just a—" he did not complete his sentence.

For an hour after the detective's departure Felix Marl sat huddled up in his chair, his head in his hands. The Crimson Circle! It was the first time he had ever been brought into even the remotest touch with that blackmailing organisation, and now its obtrusion upon the order of his thoughts was so violent that it disturbed every theory he had formed.

"I don't like it," he muttered as he got up painfully and turned on the light in the darkened room. "I think this is where I get away." He spent the evening examining his bankbook, and the examination was very comforting. He could squeeze out a little more, he thought, and then—

CHAPTER XIII

MR. MARL SQUEEZES A LITTLE MORE

ANOTHER agent of the Crimson Circle found her lines cast in pleasant places. She had been accepted by Mr. Brabazon without question, and evidently the man in the car possessed extraordinary influences.

What was even more extraordinary was that day followed day without a word from her mysterious employer. She had expected that he would almost immediately avail himself of her services, but she had been at Brabazon's (late Seller's) Bank nearly a month before she received any communication. It came one morning. She found the letter on her desk, addressed in bold pen-print.

There was no sign of the Circle on the letter, which began without preamble:

Make the acquaintance of Marl. Discover why he has a hold over Brabazon. Send me the figures of his account and notify me immediately his account is closed. Notify me also if Parr and Derrick Yale come to the bank. Wire Johnson, 23, Mildred Street, City.

She carried out her instructions faithfully, though it was not for a few days that she had an opportunity of seeing Mr. Marl.

Only once did Derrick Yale come into the bank. She had seen him before, when he was a guest of the Beardmores, and even if she had not, she would have recognised him from the portrait of the famous detective which had appeared in the newspapers.

What his business was she did not learn, but, looking out of the corner of her eye from the little office she occupied alone, by virtue of her position as Brabazon's private secretary, she saw him talking with one of the tellers at the counter, and duly notified the Crimson Circle. Inspector Parr, however, did not come, nor did she see Jack Beardmore. She did not want to think too much of Jack. He was not a pleasant subject.

In moments of perturbation John Brabazon, the austere and stately president of Seller's Bank, had a characteristic little trick. His white hands would stray to the hair, curly and thick at the back of his head. One curl he would twist about his forefinger for a moment, and then he would slowly bring the tips of his fingers across his bald dome until they rested on his forehead. In such moments, with his head bowed and his fingers resting on his brow, he had the appearance of being engaged in prayer.

The gentleman who sat with him in his neat office had no characteristics at all. He was a big man, who breathed noisily, and he was puffy with lazy, indulgent living, but he did not fidget and his hands were folded over his large waistcoat.

"My dear Marl," the banker's voice was soft and almost caressing, "you try my patience at times. I will say nothing about the strain you put upon my resources."

The big man chuckled. "I give you security, Brab—excellent security, old man. You can't deny that!"

Mr. Brabazon's white fingers played a tune on the edge of his desk.

"You bring me impossible schemes, and hitherto I have been foolish enough to finance them," he said. "There must come an end to such folly. You have no need for help. Your balance at this bank alone is nearly a hundred thousand."

Marl looked round at the door and bent forward.

"I'll tell you a story," he mumbled, "a story about a penniless young clerk that married the widow of Seller, of Seller's Bank. She was old enough to be his mother, and died suddenly—in Switzerland. She fell over a precipice. Don't I know it? Wasn't I takin' photographs of the bee-utiful mountain scenery? Did I ever show you the picture of that accident, Brab? You are in it! Yes, you're in it, though you told the examining magistrate you were miles and miles away!"

Mr. Brabazon's eyes were on the desk. Not a muscle of his face moved.

"Besides," said Mr. Marl in a more normal tone, "you can afford it. You're making another matrimonial alliance—that's the expression, ain't it?"

The banker raised his eyes and frowned at his visitor. "What do you mean?" he demanded.

Mr. Marl was evidently amused. He slapped his knee and choked with laughter.

"What about the person you met in Steyne Square the other night—the one in the closed motor-car, eh? Don't deny it! I saw you! A nice little car, it was."

Now, for the first time, Brabazon displayed signs of emotion. His face was grey and drawn and his eyes seemed to have receded further into their sockets. "I will arrange your loan," he said. Mr. Marl's expression of satisfaction was interrupted by a knock at the door. At Brabazon's "Come in," the door opened to admit one whose appearance put all other matters out of the visitor's head.

The girl brought a paper which she placed before her employer—evidently a pencilled telephone message.

"White—gold—red," Mr. Marl's senses registered the impression he received. White, creamy white and delicate skin, red as poppies the scarlet lips, yellow as ripe corn the hair. He saw her in profile, was revolted a little at the firmness of her chin—Mr. Marl liked women who were yielding and soft and malleable in his hands—but the beauty of mouth and nose and brow—they made him blink.

He breathed a little more quickly, a little more loudly, and when she had gone after a colloquy, in a low tone, he sighed.

"What a queen!" he said. "I've seen her somewhere before. What is her name?"

"Drummond—Thalia Drummond," said Mr. Brabazon, eyeing the gross man coldly.

"Thalia Drummond!" repeated Felix slowly. "Isn't she the girl who used to be with Froyant? Bit sweet on her yourself, eh, Brabazon?"

The man at the writing-table looked at the other steadily.

"I do not make it a practice to be 'sweet on' my employees, Mr. Marl," he said. "Miss Drummond is a very efficient worker. That is all that I require of my staff."

Marl rose heavily, chuckling. "I'll see you to-morrow morning about that other business," he said.

He laughed wheezily, but Mr. Brabazon did not smile. "At half-past ten to-morrow," he said, going to the door with the visitor. "Or can you make it eleven?"

"Eleven," agreed the man.

"Good morning," said the banker, but did not offer his hand. Hardly had the door closed on the visitor before Mr. Brabazon locked it and returned to his desk. He took from his pocket-book a plain white card, and dipping his pen in the red ink, drew a small circle. Beneath he wrote the words:

'Felix Marl saw our interview in Steyne Square. He lives at 79, Marisburg Place.'

He put the card into an envelope and addressed it:

'Mr. Johnson, 23, Mildred Street, City.'

CHAPTER XIV

THALIA IS ASKED OUT

MR. MARL had to pass through the bank premises, and he glanced along the two rows of desks without, however, catching a glimpse of the girl whose face he sought. Near the end of the counter was a small compartment, the occupant of which was shielded from observation by opaque glass windows. The door was ajar, and he caught just a flash of the figure and walked toward the door. A girl at a typewriter watched him curiously.

Thalia Drummond looked up from her desk to see the big smiling face of a man looking down at her.

"Busy, Miss Drummond?"

"Very," she replied, but did not seem to resent his intrusion.

"Don't get much fun here, do you?" he asked.

"Not a lot." Her dark eyes were surveying him appraisingly.

"What about a bit of dinner one of these nights and a show to follow?" he asked.

Her eyes took him in from his dyed hair to his painfully varnished boots.

"You're a wicked old man," she said calmly, "but dinner is my favourite meal."

His grin broadened and the fires of conquest flickered in his faded eyes.

"What about 'The Moulin Gris'?" He suggested the restaurant, without doubting her acceptance, but her lips curled scornfully.

"Why not at Hooligans Fish Parlour?" she asked. "No, it's the Ritz-Carlton or nothing for me."

Mr. Marl was staggered, but pleased. "You're a princess," he beamed, "and you shall have a royal feed! What about to-night?" She nodded. "Meet me at my house in Marisburg Place, Bayswater Road. 7.30. You'll find my name on the door."

He paused, expecting her to demur, but to his surprise, she nodded again.

"Good-bye, darling," said the bold Mr. Marl and kissed the tips of his fat fingers.

"Shut the door," said the girl and went on with her work.

She was destined again to be interrupted. This time the visitor was a good-looking girl, whose forearms were gauntletted in shiny leather. It was the typist who had followed Mr. Marl's movements with such curiosity.

Thalia leant back in her chair as the newcomer carefully closed the door behind her and sat down.

"Well, Macroy, what's biting you?" she asked inelegantly.

The words did not seem to harmonise with the delicate refinement of face, and not for the first time did Milly Macroy look at the girl wonderingly.

"Who's the old nut?" she asked.

"An admirer," replied Thalia calmly.

"You do attract 'em, kid," commented Milly Macroy, with some envy, and there was a little pause.

"Well?" asked Thalia. "You haven't come here to discuss my amours, have you?"

Milly smiled furtively. "If amours is French for boys, I haven't," she said. "I've come to have a straight talk with you, Drummond."

"Straight talks are meat and drink to me," said Thalia Drummond.

"Do you remember the money that went out by registered post last Friday to the Sellinger Corporation?"

Thalia nodded.

"Well, I suppose you know that they claim that when the package arrived it contained nothing but paper?"

"Is that so?" asked Thalia. "Mr. Brabazon has said nothing to me about it," and she returned the other's scrutinising glance without faltering.

"I packed that money in the envelope," said Milly Macroy slowly, "and you had it to check. There's only you and me in this business. Miss Drummond, and one of us pinched the money, and I'll swear it wasn't me."

"Then it must be me," said Thalia with an innocent smile. "Really, Macroy, that's a fairly serious accusation to make against an innocent female."

The admiration in Milly's eyes increased. "You're a Thorough-Bad, if ever there was one!" she said. "Now, look here, kid, let's put all our cards on the table. A month ago, soon after you came to the bank, there was a hundred note missing from the Foreign Exchange desk."

"Well?" asked Thalia when she paused.

"Well, I happen to know that you had it and that it was changed by you at Bilbury's in the Strand. I can tell you the number if you want to know."

Thalia swung round and looked at the other under lowered brows.

"What have we here?" she asked in mock consternation. "A female sleuth! Heavens, I am indeed undone!"

The extravagant mockery of it all took Milly aback. "You've got ice in your brain!" she said. She leant forward and laid her hand on the girl's arm. "There may be trouble over this Sellinger business, and you will want all the friends you can get."

"So will you, for the matter of that," said Thalia coolly. "You handled the money."

"And you took it," said the other, in a matter-of-fact tone. "Don't let us have any argument about it, Drummond. If we stick together there'll be no trouble at all—I can swear that the envelope was sealed in my presence and that the money was there."

There was a dancing light of amusement in Thalia Drummond's eyes and she laughed silently.

"All right," she said, with a little shrug of her shoulders. "Let it go at that. Now, I suppose, having saved me from ruin, you're going to ask me a favour? I'll set your mind at rest about the money. I took it because I had a good home for it. I need money frequently and anyway there have been lots of postal robberies lately. There was a long article in the paper about it the other day. Now go ahead."

Milly Macroy, who had not a slight acquaintance with the criminal classes, stared at the girl in amazement.

"You're ice all right," she nodded, "but you've got to cut out this cheap pilfering, otherwise you're liable to spoil a real big thing and I can't afford to see it spoilt. If you want a share of big money you've got to come in with people who are working big—do you get that?"

"I get it," said Thalia, "and who are your collaborators?"

Miss Macroy did not recognise the term but answered discreetly: "There's a gentleman I know—"

"Say 'man'," said Thalia. "Gentleman always reminds me of a tailor's ad."

"Well, a man if you like," said the patient Miss Macroy.

"He's a friend of mine and he's been watching you for a week or two, and he thinks you're the kind of clever girl who might make a lot of money without trouble. I told him about the other affair and he wants to see you."

"Another admirer?" asked Thalia Drummond with a lift of her perfect eyebrows, and Macroy's face darkened.

"There'll be none of that, you understand, Drummond," she said decisively. "This fellow and I are sort of—engaged."

"Heaven forbid," said Thalia Drummond piously, "that I should come between two loving hearts."

"And you needn't be sarcastic either," said Macroy, redder still. "I tell you that there's to be no lovey-dovey stuff in this. It's real business, you understand?"

Thalia played with her paper-knife. Presently she asked: "Suppose I don't want to come into your combination?"

Milly Macroy looked suspiciously at the girl. "Come and have a bit of dinner after the bank closes," she said.

"Nothing but invitations to dinner," murmured Thalia and the nimble-witted Milly Macroy jumped at the truth.

"The old boy asked you to dinner, did he?" she demanded. "Well, ain't that luck!" She whistled and her eyes brightened. She was about to offer a confidence, but changed her mind. "He's got loads of money out of money-lending. My dear, I can see you with a diamond necklace in a week or two!"

Thalia straightened herself and took up her pen. "Pearls are my weakness," she said. "All right, Macroy, I'll see you to-night," and she went on working.

Milly Macroy lingered. "Look here, you're not going to tell this gentleman what I said about my being engaged to him, are you?"

"There's Brab's bell," said Thalia, rising and taking up her notebook as a buzzer sounded. "No, I'm not going to discuss anything of the kind—I hate fairy stories anyway."

Miss Macroy looked after the retreating figure of the girl with an expression which was not friendly.

Mr. Brabazon was sitting at his desk when the girl came in, and handed her a scaled envelope,

"Send this by hand," he said. Thalia looked at the address and nodded, and then looked at Mr. Brabazon with a new interest. Truly the Crimson Circle was recruited from many and various classes.

CHAPTER XV

THALIA JOINS THE GANG

THALIA DRUMMOND was almost the last of the staff to leave the bank that night, and she stood on the steps looking idly from left to right as she pulled on her gloves. If she saw the man who was watching her from the opposite side of the road she did not reveal the fact by so much as a glance. Presently her eyes lighted upon Milly waiting a few yards up the street, and she walked toward her.

"You've been a long time, Drummond," grumbled Miss Macroy. "You mustn't keep my friend waiting, you know. He doesn't like it."

"He'll get over that," said Thalia. "I do not run to time-table where men arc concerned."

She fell in by Milly's side and they walked a hundred yards along the busy thoroughfare before they turned into Reeder Street.

The restaurants in Reeder Street have taken to themselves names which are designed to suggest the gaiety and epicurean wonders of Paris. The "Moulin Gris" was a small, deep shop which, with the aid of numerous mirrors and the application of gold leaf, had managed to create an atmosphere of cramped splendour.

The tables were set for dinner and empty, for it was two hours before the meal, and to the proprietors of the "Moulin Gris" such a function as afternoon tea was unknown. They went up a narrow stairway to another dining-room on the first floor, and a man who was seated at one of the tables rose briskly to meet them. He was a sleek, dark, young man, his beautifully brilliantined hair was brushed back from his forehead, and he was dressed, if not in the height of fashion, at least in the height of the fashion which he favoured.

A faint odour of l'origan, a soft large hand, a pair of bright unwinking eyes, were the first impressions which Thalia received.

"Sit down, sit down, Miss Drummond," he said brightly. "Waiter, bring that tea."

"This is Thalia Drummond," said Miss Macroy, unnecessarily it seemed.

"We needn't be introduced," laughed the young man. "I've heard a lot about you, Miss Drummond. My name's Barnet."

"'Flush' Barnet," said Thalia, and he seemed surprised and not ill-pleased. "You've heard of me, have you?"

"She's heard of everything," said Miss Macroy in resignation, "and what's more," she added significantly, "she knows Marl, and is dining with him to-night."

Barnet looked sharply from one to the other, then back again at Milly Macroy. "Have you told her anything?" he asked. There was a note of menace in his voice.

"You don't have to tell her anything," said Miss Macroy recklessly. "She knows it all!"

"Did you tell her?" he repeated.

"About Marl? No, I thought you'd tell her that."

The waiter brought the tea at that moment and there was a silence until he had gone.

"Now, I'm a plain-spoken man," said 'Flush' Barnet, "And I'm going to tell you what I call you."

"This sounds interesting," said the girl, never taking her eyes from his face.

"I call you Thorough-Bad Thalia. How's that? Good, eh?" said Mr. Barnet, leaning back in his chair and surveying her. "Thorough-Bad Thalia! You're a naughty girl! I was in court the day old Froyant charged you with pinching!" He shook his head waggishly.

"You're as full of information as last year's almanac," said Thalia Drummond coolly. "I suppose you didn't bring me here to exchange compliments?"

"No, I didn't," admitted 'Flush' Barnet, and the jealous Miss Macroy recognised, by certain signs, the fascination that the girl was casting over her lover. "I brought you here to talk business. We're all friends here, and we're all in the same old business. I want to tell you straight away that I'm not one of your little thieving crooks, who lives from hand to mouth."

He spoke very correctly, but aspirated his "h's" just a trifle heavily, Thalia duly remarked.

"I have people behind me who can find money to any amount if the job is good enough, and you're spoiling a good pitch, Thalia."

"Oh, I am, am I?" said Thalia. "Admitting I am all you think I am, in what way do I spoil the pitch?"

Mr. Barnet rolled his head from side to side with a smile. "My dear girl," he said with good-natured reproach. "How long do you think you're going to last, taking money from envelopes and sending on old bits of paper? Eh? If my friend Brabazon hadn't got the idea into his silly head that the fraud was worked in the post, you'd have had the police in your office in no time. And when I say my friend Brabazon, I'm not being funny, see?"

Here, he evidently thought he had said too much, though he found it very difficult indeed to leave the question of his friendship with the austere banker. Challenged, he might have said more, but Thalia offered no comment. "Now, I'm going to tell you something," he leant over the table and regulated his voice. "Milly and me have been working Brabazon's bank for two months. There's a big lot of money to be got, but not out of the bank—Brabazon is a friend of mine—but it can be done through one of the clients, and the man with the biggest balance is Marl."

Her lips curled for the second time that day. "That's where you're wrong," she said quietly. "Marl's balance wouldn't buy a row of beans."

He stared at her incredulously, then looked at Milly Macroy with a frown.

"You told me that he had the best part of a hundred thousand—"

"So he has," said the girl.

"He had until to-day," replied Thalia. "But this afternoon Mr. Brabazon went out—I think he went to the Bank of England, because the notes were all new. He sent for me and I saw them stacked up on his desk. He told me he was closing Marl's account, and that he was not the kind of man he wanted as a client. Then he took the money and called on Marl, I think, for when he came back just before the bank closed he handed me Marl's cheque."

"'I've settled that account, Miss Drummond,' he said. 'I don't think we'll be troubled with that blackguard again.'"

"Did he know about Marl asking you out to dinner?" asked Milly, but the girl shook her head.

Mr. Barnet said nothing. He was sitting back in his chair, fondling his chin, with a faraway look in his eyes. "A big amount, was it?" he asked.

"Sixty-two thousand," replied the girl.

"And it is in his house?" said Barnet, his face pink with excitement. "Sixty-two thousand! Did you hear that, Milly? And you're dining with him to-night?" said 'Flush' Barnet slowly and significantly. "Now, what about it?"

She met his gaze without flinching. "What about what?" she asked.

"Here's the chance of a lifetime," he said, husky with emotion. "You're going to the house. You're not above stringing the old man along, are you, Thalia?"

She was silent.

"I know the place," said 'Flush' Barnet, "one of those quaint little houses in Kensington that cost a fortune to keep up. Marisburg Place, Bayswater Road."

"I know the address pretty well," said the girl.

"He keeps three menservants," said 'Flush' Barnet, "but they're usually out any night he happens to be entertaining a lady friend. Do you get me?"

"But he's not entertaining me in his house," said the girl.

"What's the matter with a little bit of supper after the show, eh?" asked Barnet. "Suppose he puts it up to you, and you say yes. There'll be no servants in the house when you get back. That I'll take my oath. I've studied Marl."

"What do you expect me to do? Rob him?" asked Thalia. "Stick a gun under his nose and say, 'Deliver your pieces of eight'?"

"Don't be a fool," said Mr. Barnet, startled out of his pose of elegant gentleman. "You're to do nothing but have your supper and come away. Keep him amused, make him laugh. You needn't be frightened because I'll be in the house soon after you, and if there's any trouble I'll be on hand."

The girl was playing with her teaspoon, her eyes fixed on the tablecloth.

"Suppose he doesn't send his servants away?"

"You can bank on that," interrupted Mr. Barnet. "Moses! There never was such a wonderful opportunity! Do you agree?"

Thalia shook her head.

"It is too big for me. Maybe you're right and I'm likely to get into trouble, but it seems to me that petty pilfering is my long suit."

"Bah!" said Barnet in disgust. "You're mad! Now's your time to make a harvest, my dear. You're not known to the police. You're not under the limelight like me. Are you going to do it?"

She dropped her eyes again to the cloth and again fidgeted with her spoon nervously.

"All right," she said with a sudden shrug, "I might as well be hung for a sheep as a lamb."

"Or for a good share of sixty thousand as for a miserable couple of hundred, eh?" said Barnet jovially, and beckoned the waiter.

Thalia left the restaurant and turned homeward. She had to pass the bank, and it was not good policy, she thought, to hail a taxicab until she had left the neighbourhood, where Mr. Brabazon's grave eyes might observe her extravagance. She had turned into the stream of pedestrians that thronged Regent Street at this hour when she felt a touch on her arm, and turned.

A young man was walking by her side, a good-looking, keen-faced young man who did not smile ingratiatingly as others had done who had nudged her arm in Regent Street, nor did he inquire if she were going the same way as he.

"Thalia!"

She turned quickly at the sound of the voice, and for a second her self-possession failed her.

"Mr. Beardmore!" she faltered.

Jack's face was flushed and he was obviously embarrassed.

"I only wanted to speak to you for a moment. I have waited for a week for the opportunity," he said hurriedly.

"You knew I was at Brabazon's—who told you?"

He hesitated.

"Inspector Parr," he said, and when he saw the smile curl on the girl's lips, he went on: "Old Parr isn't a bad sort, really. He has never said another word against you, Thalia."

"Another!" she quoted, "but does it really matter? And now, Mr. Beardmore, I really must go. I have a very important engagement."

But he held fast to her hand.

"Thalia, won't you tell me why you did it?" he asked quietly. "Who is behind you?"

She laughed.

"There is a reason for your keeping this extraordinary company," he went on, when she stopped him.

"What extraordinary company?" she demanded.

"You have just come from a restaurant," he said. "You have been there with a man called 'Flush' Barnet, a notorious crook and a man who has served a term of penal servitude. The woman with you was Milly Macroy, a confederate of his who was concerned in the Darlington Co-Operative robbery and has also served a term of imprisonment. At present she is engaged at Brabazon's Bank."

"Well?" said the girl again.

"Surely you don't know the character of these people?" urged Jack.

"And how do you know them?" she asked calmly. "Am I wrong in supposing that you were not alone in your—vigil? Were you accompanied by the admirable Mr. Parr? I see you were. Why, you are almost a policeman yourself, Mr. Beardmore."

Jack was staggered. "Do you realise that it is Parr's duty to inform your employer that you keep that kind of company?" he asked. "For heaven's sake, Thalia, take a sane view of your position."

But she laughed. "Heaven forbid that I should interfere with the duty of a responsible police officer," she said, "but on the whole I'd rather Mr. Parr didn't. That at least is a sign of grace," she smiled. "Yes, I'd much rather he didn't. I don't mind the police speaking to me for my good because it is only right and proper that they should try to lead the weak from their sinful ways. But an employer who attempts to reform an erring girl might be a bit of a nuisance, don't you think?"

In spite of himself he laughed. "Really, Thalia, you're much too clever for the kind of company you're keeping and for the kind of life you're drifting to," he added earnestly. "I know I have no right to interfere, but perhaps I could help you. Particularly," he hesitated, "if you have done something which places you in the power of these people."

She put out her hand with a rare smile. "Good-bye," she said sweetly, and left him feeling something of a fool.

The girl walked quickly through Burlington Arcade to Piccadilly and entered a taxi. The block of mansions at which she alighted was situated in the Marylebone Road and was a distinct improvement on Lexington Street.

The liveried porter took her up in the elevator to the third floor, and she let herself into a flat which was both prettily and expensively furnished. She pressed a bell, and it was answered by a staid middle-aged woman.

"Martha," she said, "I shan't want any tea, thank you. Lay out my blue evening gown and telephone to Waltham's, Garage and tell them that I shall want a car to be here at five minutes before half past seven."

Miss Drummond's wages from the bank were exactly £4 a week.

CHAPTER XVI

MR. MARL GOES OUT

"So you've come, eh?" said Mr. Marl, rising to greet the girl. "My word, but you look smart! And you look lovely, my dear, too!"

He took both her hands in his and led her into the little gold and white drawing-room.

"Lovely!" he repeated in an almost hushed voice. "I can tell you I was a little bit scared about taking you to the Ritz-Carlton. You don't mind my frankness, do you—have a cigarette?"

He fumbled in the tail-pocket of his dress coat, produced a large gold case and opened it.

"You thought I'd turn up in one of Morne & Gillingsworth's six guinea models, eh?" she laughed as she lit the cigarette.

"Well, I did, my dear. I've had a lot of unhappy experiences," explained Marl as he seated himself heavily in an arm-chair. "I've had 'em turn up in queer clothes, I can tell you!"

"Do you make a practice of entertaining the young and the fair?" Thalia had seated herself on the big padded fireguard and was looking down at him under her half-closed lids.

"Well," said Mr. Marl complacently, rubbing his hands. "I'm not so old that I don't get some pleasure out of ladies' society. But you're stunning!"

He was a blonde, red-faced man with suspiciously brown hair, suspiciously even teeth, and for this evening he had acquired a waist which seemed wholly unreal.

"We're going to dinner and then we'll go on and see 'The Boys and the Girls' at the Winter Palace," he said, "and then," he hesitated, "what do you say to a little supper?" he asked.

"A little supper? I don't take supper," said the girl.

"Well, you can peck a bit of fruit, I suppose?" suggested Mr. Marl

"Where?" asked the girl steadily. "Most of the restaurants are closed before the theatres are out, aren't they?"

"There's no reason why you shouldn't come back here? You're not a prude, my dear, are you?"

"Not much," she confessed.

"I can see you home in my car," he said.

"I've got my own car, thank you," said the girl, and Mr. Marl's eyes opened. Then he began to laugh steadily at first, and his laughter ended in an asthmatical paroxysm. Presently he gasped: "Oh, you wicked little devil!"

The evening was an interesting one for Thalia, more interesting by reason of the fact that she caught a glimpse of Mr. 'Flush' Barnet in the hall of the hotel as she passed through.

It was after the theatre was over and they were standing in the vestibule, waiting for the lift-man to call their car, that Thalia showed some symptom of hesitation, but the eloquent Mr. Felix Marl overcame whatever reluctance she felt, and as the clock was striking the half hour after eleven she passed into the hall, not failing to notice that Mr. Marl did not ring for his servants, but let himself in with his own latchkey.

The supper was laid in a rose-panelled dining-room.

"I will help you, my dear," said Mr. Marl. "We won't bother about the servants."

But she shook her head. "I can eat nothing, and I think I'll go home now," she said.

"Wait, wait," he begged. "I want to have a little talk with you about your boss. I can do you a lot of good in that firm—at the bank, Thalia. Who called you Thalia?"

"My godfathers and godmothers, M. or N." said Thalia solemnly, and Mr. Marl squeaked his delight at her humour.

He was passing behind her, ostensibly to reach one of the dishes which were set on the table, when he stooped and, had she not slipped from his grasp, would have kissed her. "I think I'll go home," said Thalia.

"Rubbish!" Mr. Marl was annoyed, and when Mr. Marl was annoyed he forgot that he made any pretensions to gentle birth. "Come and sit down."

She looked at him long and thoughtfully, and then, turning suddenly, went to the door, and turned the handle. It was locked.

"I think you had better open this door, Mr. Marl," she said quietly.

"I think not," chuckled Mr. Marl. "Now, Thalia, be the dear, good little girl I thought you were."

"I should hate to dissipate any illusions you may have about my character," said Thalia coolly. "You'll open that door, please."

"Certainly,"

He ambled toward the door, feeling in his pocket, then before she could realise his intention he had seized her in his arms. He was a powerful man, a head taller than she, and his big hands gripped her arms like steel clamps.

"Let me go," said Thalia steadily. She did not lose her nerve nor show the least sign of fear.

Suddenly he felt her tense muscles relax. He had conquered.

With a quick intake of breath he released his hold of the sullen girl.

"Let me have some supper," she said, and he beamed.

"Now, my dear, you are being the little girl I—what's that?"

The last was a squeak of terror.

She had strolled slowly to the table and had taken up the brocade bag. He had watched her and thought she was seeking a handkerchief. Instead she had produced a small, black, egg-shaped thing, and with a flick of her left hand had pulled out a small pin and dropped the pin on to the table. He knew what it was—he had dabbled in army supplies and had seen many Mills bombs.

"Put it down—no, no, put the pin in, you young fool!" he whimpered.

"Don't worry," she said coolly. "I have a spare pin in my bag—open that door!"

His hand shook like a man with palsy as he fumbled at the keyhole. Then he turned and blinked at her.

"A Mills bomb!" he mumbled, and fell back an obese mass of quivering flesh against the delicate panelling.

Slowly she nodded. "A Mills bomb," she said softly, and went out, still gripping the lever of the deadly egg-like thing. He followed her to the door and slammed it after he, then went shakily up the stairs to his bedroom.

"Flush" Barnet, standing in the shadow of a clothes-press, heard the click of locks and the snap of a bolt as Mr. Marl entered his room. The house was still. Through the thick door of Mr. Marl's bedroom no sound came. There was no transom to the door, and the only evidence that there was somebody in his room was afforded by a fret of light in the ceiling of the passage, which came through a ventilator in the wall of the bedroom.

During the war this house had been used as an officers' convalescent home, and certain hygienic arrangements had been introduced, which were more useful than beautiful.

'Flush' crept softly in his stockinged feet to the door and listened. He thought he heard the man talking to himself and looked around for some means by which he could obtain a view of the room. There was a small oaken table in the corridor and he placed this against the wall and mounted. His eyes came to the level of the ventilator and he looked down upon Mr. Marl pacing the room in his shirt-sleeves, obviously disturbed. Then 'Flush' Barnet heard a sound. Just a faint "hush-hush" of feet on a carpet, and he slipped down, walked quickly along the corridor, passing the head of the stairs.

The hall below was in darkness, but he felt rather than saw a figure on the stairway. Whether it was man or woman he could not say, and did not stop to discover. It might be one of the servants returning furtively—servants did not always stay away when they were bidden. 'Flush' passed to the farther end of the corridor and from an angle in the wall watched. He saw nobody pass the head of the stairs, but there was no background. After a while he crept back again. There was nothing to be gained by forcing the door of Marl's bedroom, even if it were possible. He had had time to inspect the house at his leisure, and he had already decided upon investigating the little safe in the library, for Mr. Marl's own room had drawn blank.

The "investigation", which took two hours and the employment of one of the best sets of tools in the profession, was not unprofitable. But it did not reveal the huge sum of money which he anticipated. He hesitated. The night was too far through to make an attempt on the bedroom, even if he had not already searched it from wall to wall. He folded his kit and slipped it into one pocket, his loot into another, and went upstairs again. There was no sound from Marl's room, but the light was still on. He tried to look through the keyhole, but the key was still there. The only inducement there was for him to enter the room was the possibility that the money was in the man's clothes. This likelihood was remote, he thought. Possibly Marl had taken it to some safe deposit—a contingency which Barnet had foreseen.

He went slowly down the stairs, through the hall and the butler's pantry to the side door, where he had left his boots, his overcoat and his shiny silk hat, for he was in evening dress. Then he stole softly forth along the covered passageway running by the side of the house. Here a door opened into the little forecourt of Marl's house.

He reached the garden and his hand was on the gate when somebody touched him and he spun round.

"I want you, 'Flush'," said a well-remembered voice. "Inspector Parr. You may remember me?"

"Parr!" gasped the bewildered Barnet, and with an oath wrenched himself free and leapt through the gate, but the three policemen who were waiting for him were not so easy to dispose of, and they marched 'Flush' Barnet to the nearest police station, a worried man.

In the meantime Parr conducted a search of his own. Accompanied by a detective he made his way to the hall of the house and up the stairs.

"This is the only room occupied apparently," he said, and knocked at the door.

There was no reply. "Go along and see if you can rouse any of the servants," said Parr.

The man came back with the startling information that there were no servants in the house.

"There's somebody here," said the old inspector, and flashing his lamp along the corridor he saw the table, and with an agility remarkable in one of his age, he leapt up and peered through the ventilator.

"I can just see somebody asleep," he said. "Hi! Wake up!" he called, but there was no reply. Hammering on the door did not produce any response.

"Go down and see if you can find a hatchet, we'll break open the door," said Parr. "I don't like this." Hatchet there was none, but they found a hammer, "Can you show a light, Mr. Parr?" asked the man, and the inspector flashed his lamp on the door. It was a white door—white except for the Crimson Circle affixed to a panel as by a rubber stamp.

"Break in the door," said Parr, breathing heavily.

For five minutes they smashed at a panel before they finally hammered it through, and the sleeper within gave no sign of consciousness.

Parr reached his hand through the door, turned the key and, by dint of stretching, found the bolt at the top. He slipped into the room. The light was still burning and its rays fell across the man on the bed, who lay upon his back, a twisted smile on his face, most obviously dead.

CHAPTER XVII –

THE BLOWER OF BUBBLES

IT was long after midnight and Derrick Yale was sitting in his pretty little study—he lived in a flat overlooking the park—when the knock came to the door and he rose to admit Inspector Parr.

Parr related the incident of the evening. "But why didn't you tell me?" asked Derrick a little reproachfully, and then laughed. "I'm sorry," he said. "I always seem to be butting in on your affairs. But how came the murderer to escape? You say you had had the house surrounded for two hours. Did the girl come out?"

"Undoubtedly; she came out and drove home."

"And nobody else went in?"

"I wouldn't like to swear that," said Parr. "Whoever was in the house had probably arrived long before Marl returned from the theatre. I have since discovered that there was a way out through the garage at the back of the house. When I said the house was surrounded that was an exaggeration. There was a way through the back garden which I did not know. I didn't even suspect there were gardens there. Undoubtedly he went through the garage door."

"Do you suspect the girl at all?" Parr shook his head. "But why were you surrounding Marl's house at all?" asked Derrick Yale seriously.

The answer was as unexpected as it was sensational.

"Because Marl has been under police observation ever since he came back to London," said Parr. "In fact, ever since I discovered that he was the man who wrote the letter, the scrap of which I found and which I compared last week with his writing—I asked him for the address of his tailor."

"Marl?" said the other incredulously.

Inspector Parr nodded.

"I don't know what there was between old man Beardmore and Marl, or what brought him to the house. I've been trying to reconstruct the scene. You may remember that when Marl came to the house on a visit he was suddenly seized with a panic."

"I remember," nodded Yale. "Jack Beardmore told me about it. Well?"

"He refused to stay at the house, said he was going back to London," said Parr. "As a matter of fact, he went no farther than Kingside, which is a station some eight or nine miles away. He sent his bag on to London and came back by road. He was probably the person whom the murderer saw in the wood that night. Now why had he come back if he was so scared that he ran away in the first place? And why did he write that letter for delivery in the night when he had every opportunity to tell James Beardmore by day, when he was with him?"

There was a long silence. "How was Marl killed?" asked Yale.

The other shook his head. "That is a mystery to me. The murderer could not possibly have entered the room. I had an interview with 'Flush' Barnet—as yet he knows nothing about the murder—and he admits he broke in for the purpose of burglary. He says he heard the sound of somebody moving about the house, and very naturally hid himself. He also says he heard a strange hissing sound, like air escaping from a pipe. Another remarkable clue was a round wet patch on the pillow, within a few inches of the dead man's hand. It was exactly circular. At first I thought it was a symbol of the Crimson Circle, until I discovered another patch on the counterpane. The doctor has not been able to diagnose the cause of death, but the motive is clear. According to his banker—I've just been talking to Brabazon on the telephone—he drew a large sum of money from the bank yesterday. In fact, Brabazon closed his account. They had a quarrel over something or other. The safe was of course opened by 'Flush' Barnet, but there was no money found on him when he was searched at the police station. Curiously enough, we did discover several little oddments that 'Flush' had picked up—now, who took the money?"

Derrick Yale paced the floor, his hands behind him, his chin on his breast. "Do you know anything of Brabazon?" he asked.

The other did not reply immediately. "Only that he is a banker and does a lot of foreign work."

"Is he solvent?" asked Derrick Yale bluntly, and the inspector raised his dull eyes slowly until they were on a level with the other's.

"No," he said, "and I don't mind telling you that we've had one or two complaints about his methods."

"Were they good friends—Marl and Brabazon?"

"Fairly good," was the hesitating reply. "The impression I have from reports is that Marl had some hold over Brabazon."

"And Brabazon was insolvent," mused Derrick Yale. "And this afternoon Marl closes his account. In what circumstances? Did he come to the bank?"

Briefly the detective explained what had happened. It seemed that there was precious little that did happen at Brabazon's bank that he did not know.

Derrick Yale was beginning to respect this man, whom at first he had regarded, with a good-natured scorn, as a little stupid.

"I wonder if it would be possible for me to go to Marl's house to-night?"

"I came to suggest that," said the other. "In fact, I kept a cab waiting at the door with that idea."

Derrick Yale did not speak during the journey to Bayswater, and it was not until he stood in the hall of the house in Marisburg Place that he broke the silence.

"We ought to find a small steel cylinder somewhere," he said slowly.

The policeman standing on duty in the hall came forward and saluted the inspector.

"We found an iron bottle in the garage, sir?" he said.

"Ah!" cried Derrick Yale triumphantly. "I thought so!"

He almost ran up the stairs ahead of the detective and paused in the passage, which was now lighted. The little oak table stood against the ventilator and toward that he moved. Then he went down on his hands and knees and sniffed the carpet. Presently he choked and coughed and got up, red in the face.

"Let me see that cylinder," he said. They brought it to him. The policeman's description of it as a bottle was nearer the truth. It was an iron bottle, at the end of which was a small pipe to which was attached a tiny turn-key.

"And now there ought to be a cup somewhere," he said, looking round, "unless he brought it in a bottle."

"There was a small glass bottle in the garage near this, sir," said the policeman who had found it, "it is broken, though."

"Bring it to me quickly," said Yale. "And I can only hope that it isn't so completely smashed that none of its contents are left."

The stout Mr. Parr was regarding him sombrely.

"What is all this about?" he asked, and Derrick Yale chuckled.

"A new way of committing a murder, my dear Mr. Parr," he said airily, "now let us go into the room."

The body of Marl lay on the bed covered by a sheet and the circular patch of wet on the pillow had not dried. The windows were open and a fitful wind kept the curtains fluttering.

"Of course you can't smell it here," said Yale speaking to himself, and again went on his knees and nosed the carpet. And again he coughed and rose hurriedly.

By this time they had returned with the lower half of a glass bottle. It contained a few drops of liquid, and this Yale poured into his hand.

"Soap and water," he said; "I thought it would be. And now I'll explain how Marl was killed. Your thief, 'Flush' Barnet, heard a hissing sound. It was the sound of a heavy gas escaping from this cylinder. I may be wrong, but I should imagine there is enough poison gas in that little iron bottle to settle your account and mine. It is still lying on the floor, by the way. It is one of those heavy gases which descend."

"But how did it kill Marl? Did they pump it through the grating on to his head?"

Derrick Yale shook his head. "It is a much simpler and a much more deadly method which the Crimson Circle employed," he said quietly.

"They blew bubbles."

"Bubbles?"

Derrick Yale nodded. "The end of this cylinder—you can still feel the slime of the soap upon it—was first dipped into the soap solution, then thrust through the grating. The tap was turned down and a bubble formed, which was shaken off. From the ventilator," he ran outside and jumped on to the table, "yes, I thought so," he said, "he could see Marl's head. Two or three of the bubbles must have been failures. One struck the pillow, but I should imagine that that was blown after his death; one struck the wall, you will find the wet patch, but one, and probably more, burst on his face. He must have been killed almost instantaneously." Parr could only gape. "I thought it all out on the way here. The circular patch on the pillow reminded me of my own boyish exploits and their disastrous effect when I started blowing bubbles in the bedroom. And then when you mentioned the ventilator and the hissing noise, I was perfectly certain that my theory was right."

"But we smelt no gas when we came into the room," said Parr.

"The wind may have blown away the fumes," said Derrick Yale. "But apart from that, the weight of the gas would send it to the floor, and by its own density it would spread evenly—look!" He struck a match, shielded it for a moment until it caught light, and then slowly brought it to the floor level. An inch from the carpet the match was suddenly extinguished.

"I see," said Inspector Parr.

"Now what about searching the place? Perhaps I can be of use," suggested Yale, but his offer of help did not meet with any very gracious response.

A small police audience, which had listened awe-stricken while Yale had developed his theory, could understand the Inspector's feelings. Apparently Yale did, too, for with a good-humoured laugh he made his excuses and went home. There are moments when the head-quarters police should be left alone with their own emotions. Nobody realised this more than Derrick Yale.

CHAPTER XVIII

'FLUSH' BARNET'S STORY

INSPECTOR PARR, after a further search, proceeded to the nearest police station to interview Mr. 'Flush' Barnet.

'Flush', a depressed and weary man, had no illuminating information to give.

The proceeds of his robbery lay upon the station-sergeant's table, a miscellaneous collection of rings and watches, a perfectly valueless bank-book—valueless to 'Flush', at any rate—and a silver flask. But the most surprising circumstance was that in 'Flush' Barnet's pocket were two brand new bank notes for a hundred pounds, which he insisted stoutly were his own property.

Now burglars, and particularly the type of burglar that 'Flush' Barnet was, are notoriously improvident people. They do not work whilst they have money, and with two hundred pounds in his possession, it is certain that 'Flush' Barnet would not have attempted to break into Marisburg Place.

"They're my own, I tell you, Mr. Parr," he protested. "Would I tell you a lie?"

"Of course you would," said Inspector Parr without heat. "If they are your own, where did you get them?"

"They were given to me by a friend."

"Why did you light a fire in the library?" asked Parr unexpectedly, and 'Flush' Barnet started. "Because I was cold," he said after a pause. "H'm," said Inspector Parr, and then as though speaking his thoughts aloud, "he has two hundred of his own, he breaks into a house, he burgles a safe and lights a fire. Now, why did he light the fire? Why did he light the fire? To burn something he'd found in the safe!"

'Flush' Barnet listened without offering any comment, but he was visibly distressed.

"Therefore," said Parr, "you were paid to break into Marl's house and you got two hundred for pinching something from his safe and burning it. Am I right?"

"If I died this moment—" began 'Flush' Barnet.

"You'd go to hell," said the inspector dispassionately, "where all liars go. Who is your pal, Barnet? You'd better tell me, because I'm in two minds whether I shall charge you with the murder—"

"Murder!" almost screamed 'Flush' Barnet, as he sprang to his feet. "What do you mean? I haven't committed a murder!"

"Marl's dead, that's all; found dead in his bed."

He left the prisoner in a state of mental prostration, and when he returned in the early hours of the morning to renew his inquisition, 'Flush' Barnet told him all. "I don't know anything about Crimson Circles, Mr. Parr," he said, "but this is the truth."

He added a pious wish that Providence would deal hardly with him if he departed from veracity.

"I'm keeping company with a young lady at Brabazon's bank. One night when she was working late, I was waiting for her when a gentleman came out of the side entrance of the bank and called me. I was surprised to hear him mention my name, and I nearly dropped dead when I saw his face."

"It was Mr. Brabazon?" suggested Parr.

"That's right, sir. He asked me into his private office. I thought he'd got something against Milly."

"Go on," said Parr, when the man paused.

"Well, I've got to save myself, haven't I? And I suppose I'd better speak the whole truth. He told me that Marl was blackmailing him, and that Marl had some letters of his which he kept in his private safe, and offered me a thousand if I'd get them. That's the truth. And then he gave me an idea that Marl kept a lot of money in the house. He didn't exactly say so, but that is what he hinted. He knew I'd been inside for burglary, he'd made inquiries about me, and said that I was the right kind of man. Well, sir, I went round and took a squint at the place, and it seemed to me that it was a bit difficult. There were always men servants in the house, except when Mr. Marl was entertaining ladies to supper," he grinned. "I'd have given up the job, only there's a young lady in the office that Marl was sweet on."

"Thalia Drummond?" suggested Parr.

"That's right, sir," nodded 'Flush'. "It was what you might call an act of Providence, him being sweet on her, and when I found that he'd invited her to dinner, I thought that was a good opportunity to get in. It seemed money for nothing when I found out that he'd drawn his bank balance. I opened the safe—that was easy—found the envelope, but it had no papers, only a photograph of a man and a woman on a rock. I think it was a photograph of some place abroad, for there were lots of mountains in the background, and he seemed to be pushing her over and she was holding on to a bit of tree. Maybe it was one of those cinema pictures. Anyway, I burnt it."

"I see," said Inspector Parr. "And that is all?"

"That's all, sir. I never found any money."

At seven o'clock, with a warrant in his pocket, and accompanied by two detectives, Inspector Parr made a call at the block of flats where Brabazon had his residence.

A servant in night attire opened the door to them and indicated the banker's room. The door was locked, but Parr kicked it open without ceremony. The room, however, was empty. An open window and a fire escape suggested the method by which the eminent banker had made his getaway, and the fact that the bed had not been slept in and that there was no sign of disorder in the room, showed that he had gone hours before the detective's arrival.

By the side of the bed there was a telephone, and Parr called the exchange.

"Can you find if any message came through to this number during the night?" he asked. "I am Inspector Parr, of police head-quarters."

"Two," was the reply. "I put them through myself. One from Bayswater—"

"That was mine," said the Inspector. "What was the other?"

"From the Western Exchange—at 2.30."

"Thank you," said the inspector grimly, and hung up the telephone.

He looked at his companions and rubbed his big nose irritably.

"Thalia Drummond is going to get another job," he said.

CHAPTER XIX

THALIA ACCEPTS AN OFFER

IT took over a week to settle the preliminaries of Brabazon's insolvency, and at the end of that time, Thalia walked from the bank with a week's salary in her little leather bag, and no immediate prospects of employment.

Inspector Parr had not minced his words, which he had addressed to her before an impressed audience.

"Only the fact that I saw you come out of Marl's house and saw him close the door on you, saves you from a serious charge," he said.

"If it had only saved me from a lecture also, I should have been pleased," said Thalia coolly.

"What do you make of her?" asked Parr, as the girl disappeared through the swing doors of the office.

"She rather puzzles me," It was Derrick Yale to whom he had addressed his question. "And the more I think of her, the more I am puzzled. The woman Macroy says that she has been engaged in pilfering since she has been at the bank, but there is no proof of that. In fact, the only person who could supply the proof is our absent friend, Brabazon. Why didn't you call her as a witness in the prosecution of Barnet?"

"It would be a case of Barnet's word against hers," said the detective, shaking his head, "and the case against Barnet was so clear that I didn't want any further evidence than my own eyes."

Yale was frowning thoughtfully. "I wonder," he said, half to himself.

"What do you wonder?"

"I wonder if this girl could give us a little more information about the Crimson Circle than we have at present. I'm half inclined to engage her." Parr muttered something under his breath. "I know you think I'm mad, but really I have method in my madness. There is nothing to steal in my office; she would be under my eye all the time, and if she were in communication with the Circle, I should certainly know all about it. Besides, she interests me."

"Why did you shake hands with her?" asked Parr curiously, and the other laughed.

"That is why she interests me. I wanted to get an impression, and the impression I had was of some dark sinister force in the background of her life. That girl is not working independently. She has behind her—"

"The Crimson Circle?" suggested Parr, and there was the suggestion of a sneer in his tone.

"Very likely," said the other seriously. "Anyway, I'm going to see her." He called at Thalia's flat that afternoon, and her servant showed him into the pretty little drawing-room. A minute after Thalia came in, and there was a smile in her fine eyes as she recognised her visitor.

"Well, Mr. Yale, have you come to give me a few words of warning?"

"Not exactly," laughed Yale. "I've come to offer you a job."

Her eyebrows rose. "Do you want an assistant," she asked ironically, "acting on the principle that to catch a thief you must employ a thief? Or have you views about my reformation? Several people want to reform me," she said. She sat down on the piano stool, her hands behind her, and he knew that she was mocking him.

"Why do you steal, Miss Drummond?"

"Because it is my nature to," she said without hesitation. "Why should kleptomania be confined to the ruling classes?"

"Do you get any satisfaction out of it?" he demanded. "I'm not asking out of idle curiosity, but as a student of human man and woman."

She waved her hand round the apartment. "I have the satisfaction of a very comfortable home," she said. "I have a good servant, and I am not likely to starve. All these things are particularly satisfying to me. Now tell me about the job, Mr. Yale. Do you want me to be a policewoman?"

"Not exactly," he smiled, "but I want a secretary, somebody upon whom I can rely. My work is increasing at a tremendous rate; my correspondence is much more than I can cope with. I will add, that there is little opportunity in my office for the exercise of your pet vice," he added good-humouredly, "and anyway, I'll take that risk."

She considered a moment, looking at him steadily. "If you're willing to take the risk, so am I," she said at last. "Where is your office?" He gave her the address. "I shall be with you at ten o'clock in the morning. Lock up your cheque-book and clear away your loose change," she said.

"A remarkable girl," he thought as he was going back to the city.

He spoke no more than the truth when he had told Parr that she puzzled him, and yet he had met with every type of criminal, and probably knew more of criminal psychology than did Parr with all his experience.

His mind strayed to Parr, that unhappy individual whom he knew was in disgrace. How much longer would police head-quarters tolerate him after this third failure to deal with the Crimson Circle, he wondered.

Mr. Parr was thinking on the same lines that night. A brief official memo, had awaited him on his arrival at headquarters, and he read it with a grimace of pain. And there was worse to follow, he guessed, and he had good reason for that fear. The next morning he was summoned to the house of Mr. Froyant, and found Derrick Yale already there.

For all their good relationship, the chase of the Crimson Circle had developed into a duel between these strangely different personalities. It was an open secret in newspaper land that Parr's impending ruin was due less to the unchecked villainies of the Crimson Circle, than to the superhuman brilliancy of this unofficial rival. To do him justice, Yale did his best to discredit this view, but it was held.

Froyant, for all his meanness and his knowledge of Yale's heavy fees, had commissioned him immediately after he had received the warning. His faith in the police had evaporated, and he made no attempt to disguise his scepticism.

"Mr. Froyant has decided to pay," were the words which greeted the inspector.

"Eh, of course I shall pay!" exploded Mr. Froyant.

He had aged ten years in the past few days, thought Parr; his face was white, and thinner, and he seemed to have shrunk within himself.

"If police head-quarters allow this dastardly association to threaten respectable citizens, and cannot even protect their lives, what else is there to be done, but to pay. My friend Pindle has had a similar threat, and he has paid. I cannot stand the strain of this any longer."

He paced up and down the library floor like a man demented.

"Mr. Froyant will pay," said Derrick Yale slowly. "But this time I think the Crimson Circle have been just a little too venturesome."

"What do you mean?" asked Parr.

"Have you the letter, sir?" demanded Yale, and Froyant pulled open a drawer savagely and slammed down the familiar card upon his blotting-pad.

"When did this arrive?" asked Parr as he took it up, noting the Crimson Circle. "By this morning's post."

Parr read the words inscribed in the centre:

'We shall call for the money at the office of Mr. Derrick Yale at 3.30 on Friday afternoon. The notes must not run in series. If it is not there for us, you will die the same night.'

Three times the inspector read the short message, and then he sighed.

"Well, that simplifies matters," he said. "Of course, they will not call—"

"I think they will," said Yale quietly; "but I shall be prepared for them, and I should like you to be on hand, Mr. Parr."

"If there is one thing more certain that another," said the inspector phlegmatically, "it is that I shall be on hand. But I don't think they will come."

"There I can't agree with you," said Yale. "Whoever the central figure of the Crimson Circle is, he or she does not lack courage. And, by the way," he lowered his voice, "you will meet an old acquaintance at my office."

Parr shot a quick, suspicious glance at the detective, and saw that he was mildly amused. "Drummond?" he asked. Yale nodded. "You are engaging her?"

"She rather interests me, and I fancy that she is going to be a real help in the solution of this mystery."

Froyant came in at that moment, and, the conversation was tactfully changed.

CHAPTER XX

THE KEY OF RIVER HOUSE

IT was arranged that Froyant should draw the necessary money from his bank on the Thursday morning to pay the demand, and that Yale should call for it and meet Parr at the former's office in ample time to make the necessary preparations for the visitor's reception.

Mr. Parr's way to head-quarters took him past the big house where Jack Beardmore was living in solitude.

The events of the past few weeks had wrought an extraordinary change in the youth. From a boy he had suddenly become a man, with all a man's balance and understanding. He had inherited an enormous fortune, but with its coming the incentive of life had, for the most part, fallen away. He could never escape the memory of Thalia Drummond; her face was before him, sleeping or waking, and though he called himself a fool, and could, as he did, argue the matter to a logical conclusion, the sum of all his reasoning faded before the image he carried in his heart.

Between Inspector Parr and he there had grown a curious friendship. There was a time when he was near to hating the stout little man, but his good sense had told him that however large a part sentiment had played in his own life, and in the direction of his own actions, it could have no place in a police officer's moral equipment.

The inspector stopped before the door of the house, and was for passing on, but, obeying an impulse, he walked slowly up the steps and rang the bell. The footman who admitted him was one of the dozen servants who accentuated the emptiness of the mansion.

Jack was in the dining-room, pretending to be interested in a late breakfast.

"Come in, Mr. Parr," he said, rising. "I suppose you breakfasted hours ago. Is there anything new?"

"Nothing," said Parr, "except that Mr. Froyant has decided to pay."

"He would," said Jack contemptuously, and then, for the first time in a long while, he laughed. "I shouldn't like to be the Red or Crimson Circle, or whatever it calls itself."

"Why not?" asked Mr. Parr, with a little light of amusement in his eyes, but he could guess the answer.

"My poor father used to say that Froyant fretted over every cent that was taken from him and never rested until he got it back. When Harvey's panic is over he will go after the Crimson Circle, and will never leave it until every banknote he has handed to them is repaid."

"Very likely," agreed the inspector, "but they aren't holding the money yet." He told Jack the contents of the letter which Froyant had received that morning, and his young host was visibly astonished.

"They're taking a big risk, aren't they? It would be a clever man who got the better of Derrick Yale."

"So I think," said the inspector, crossing his legs comfortably. "I must take my hat off to Yale. There are things about him that I admire tremendously."

"His psychometrical powers, for example," smiled Jack, but the inspector shook his head.

"I don't know enough about those to admire them. They seem uncanny to me, yet in a certain way I can understand them. No, I am thinking of other of his qualities."

He was suddenly silent, and Jack sensed his depression.

"You're having a pretty bad time at head-quarters, aren't you?" he asked. "I don't suppose they are particularly pleased with the immunity of the Crimson Circle?"

Parr nodded.

"I'm not exactly in a bed of roses just now," he admitted. "But that doesn't worry me a bit." He looked steadily at Jack. "By the way, your young friend is in a new job."

Jack started. "My young friend?" he stammered. "You mean Miss—"

"Miss Drummond, I mean. Derrick Yale has engaged her," he chuckled softly at Jack's astonishment.

"Engaged Miss Thalia Drummond? You're joking, surely?" said Jack.

"I thought he was joking when he suggested it. He's a queer bird, is Yale."

"He ought to be at head-quarters, a lot of people think," said Jack, and realised that he had made a faux pas before the words were out.

But if Mr. Parr was hurt he did not show it.

"They don't take them in from outside," he said with a smile, and the inspector very rarely smiled. "Otherwise, Mr. Beardmore, we should have taken you! No, our friend is clever. I suppose you don't expect a head-quarters' man to admit that what we call a 'fancy' detective can be anything but an interfering fool? But Yale is clever."

They had strolled together to the window, and were looking out into the sedate street in which Jack Beardmore's residence was situated.

"Isn't that Miss Drummond?" he asked suddenly.

Parr had already seen her. She was walking slowly along the other side of the road, looking at the numbers of the houses. Presently she crossed.

"She's coming here," gasped Jack. "I wonder what—" He did not wait to finish what he had to say, but rushed out of the room and opened the hall door to her whilst her finger was lingering on the bell push.

"It is good to see you, Thalia," he said, gripping her warmly by the hand. "Won't you come in? An old acquaintance of yours is in the dining-room."

She raised her eyebrows. "Not Mr. Parr?"

"You're a wonderful guesser," laughed Jack as he closed the door behind her. "Did you want to see me alone?" he asked suddenly.

She shook her head.

"No; I've only a message for you from Mr. Yale. He wanted you to let him have the key of your riverside house."

By this time they were in the dining-room, and the girl, meeting the expressionless gaze of Mr. Parr, nodded curtly.

"You evidently do not love my friend, Mr. Parr," thought Jack.

He explained the object of the girl's visit.

"My poor father had a derelict property by the riverside," he said. "It has not been tenanted for years, and the surveyors tell me it will cost almost as much as the property is worth to put it into repair. For some reason Yale thinks that Brabazon will use this as a hiding-place. Brabazon had it in his hands for some time, trying to sell it. He looked after some of my father's property. But is he at all likely to be there?"

Mr. Parr pursed his large lips and blinked meditatively.

"The only thing I know about him is that so far he has not left the country," he said at last. "I should not think he'd go to a house which he must know would be searched." He stared absently at Thalia. "Yet he might," he mused. "I suppose he has a key to the place. What is it, a house?"

"It is half house and half warehouse," said Jack. "I have never seen it, but I believe it is one of those dwellings which the old merchants favoured two hundred years ago, in the days when they lived in the places where they carried on business."

He unlocked his desk and pulled out a drawer full of keys, each bearing a label.

"This is the one, I think, Miss Drummond," he said, handing the key to her. "How do you like your new job?"

It required some courage to ask the question, for he was almost awestricken in her presence.

She smiled faintly.

"It is amusing," she said, "without being in any way tempting! I cannot tell you very much about it, because I only started this morning." She turned to the detective. "'No, I shan't trouble you very much, Mr. Parr," she said. "The only thing of value in the office is a silver paper-weight—I don't even have to post the letters," she went on mockingly. "The office is, built on the American plan, and there is a little chute in Mr. Yale's private office that drops the letters straight away into the box in the hall below. It is very disappointing!"

Solemn though she was, her eyes were dancing with merriment.

"You're a queer woman, Thalia Drummond," said Parr, "and yet I'm sure there is some good in you."

The remark seemed to cause her unbounded amusement. She laughed until the tears were in her eyes, and Jack grinned sympathetically.

Parr, on the other hand, showed no sign of amusement.

"Be careful," he said ominously, and the smile faded from her lips.

"You may be sure I shall be very careful, Mr. Parr," she said, "and if I am in any kind of trouble, you can be equally sure that I shall send immediately for you!"

"I hope you will," said Parr, "though I have my doubts."

CHAPTER XXI

RIVER HOUSE

THALIA went straight back to the office and found Derrick Yale sitting in his room reading through a heap of unanswered correspondence.

"Is that the key? Thank you. Put it down there," he said. "I am afraid you will have to answer most of these yourself. The majority of them are from foolish young people who wish to be trained as private detectives. You will find a form reply, and you can sign the answers yourself. And will you tell this lady," he handed a letter across to her, "that I am so busy now that I cannot undertake any further commissions?"

He took up the key from the table and held it for a second on his hand.

"You saw Mr. Parr?"

She laughed.

"You're almost terrifying, Mr. Yale. I did see Mr. Parr, but how did you know?"

He shook his head smilingly.

"It is really very simple, and I should take no credit for my gift," he said, "any more than you take credit for your good looks and your predisposition to—shall I say 'take things as you find them'?"

She did not answer at once, then: "I am a reformed character."

"I believe you will reform in time. You interest me," said Yale, and then, after a pause, "immensely!" And with a jerk of his head he dismissed her.

She was in the midst of her work and her typewriter was clacking furiously when he appeared at the door of his room.

"Will you try to get Mr. Parr on the telephone?" he said. "You will find his number on the register."

Mr. Parr was not in his office when she called, but half an hour later she reached him, and switched through the wire to the next room.

"Is that you, Parr?"

She heard his voice through the door, which was left ajar.

"I am going to Beardmore's river property to make a search. I have an idea that Brabazon may be hiding there! After lunch; all right. Will you be here at half-past two?"

Thalia Drummond listened and made a shorthand note on her blotting-pad.

At half-past two Parr called. She did not see him, for there was a direct entrance to Yale's room from the corridor without, but she heard the rumble of his voice, and presently they went out.

She waited until their footsteps had died away, then she took a telegraph form, and addressing it to Johnson, 23, Mildred Street, City, she wrote:

'Derrick Yale has gone to search Beardmore's riverside house.'

Thalia Drummond was nothing if not dutiful.

The house stood upon a little wharf, and was a picture of desolation and neglect. The stone foundation of the wharf was in decay, the parapet broken, the yard a wilderness of weed; rank grasses and nettles formed almost an impenetrable barrier to their progress after they had opened the gate which led from the mean east-end street in which the wharfage was cited.

The house itself might at one time have been picturesque, but now, with its broken lower windows, its weather-stained woodwork and discoloured walls, it was a pitiable piece of architectural wreckage.

At one end was a big, gaunt, stone store, built flush with the wharf's edge, and apparently communicating with the house. An air-raid during the war had demolished one comer of the wall, and robbed it of a few slates which remained, leaving the skeleton of rotting roof ribs nakedly bare to inspection.

"A cheerful place," said Yale, as he opened the door. "It is not the sort of setting in which one could imagine the elegant Brabazon, is it?"

The passage-way was dusty. Cobwebs hung from the ceiling and the house was silent and lifeless. They made a rapid tour through the rooms, without, however, discovering any sign of the fugitive.

"There is a garret here," said Yale, pointing to a flight of steps that led to a trap-door in the ceiling of the upper floor.

He ran up the steps, pushed open the flap and disappeared. Parr-heard him walking along and presently he came down.

"Nothing there," he said as he slammed the trap-door in its place.

"I never expected that you would find anything," said Parr as he led the way out of the house.

They crossed the weed-grown path to the outer gate, and from a garret window a white-faced man watched them through the dusty glass; a man with a week's growth of beard, whom even his most intimate friends would never have recognised as Mr. Brabazon, the well-known banker,

CHAPTER XXII

THE MESSENGER OF THE CIRCLE

"YOU'RE a fool, sir, and an idiot. I thought you were a clever detective, but you're a fool!"

Mr. Froyant was in his most savage mood, and the neat stack of bank-notes which stood upon his desk supplied the reason.

The sight of so much good money going away from him was a cause of unspeakable anguish to the miserly Harvey, and if his eyes strayed away from that accumulation of wealth, they came back again almost instantly.

Derrick Yale was a difficult man to offend.

"Perhaps I am," he said, "but I must run my own business in my own way, Mr. Froyant, and if I think that the girl can lead me to the Crimson Circle—as I do think—then I shall employ her."

"Mark my words," Froyant shook his fingers in the detective's face, "that girl is with the gang. You will discover, my friend, that she is the messenger who will call for the money!"

"In which case she will be immediately arrested," said the other. "Believe me, Mr. Froyant, I have no intention of losing sight of these notes, but if they are taken by the Crimson Circle, the responsibility must be mine not yours. My job is to save your life, and to divert the vengeance of the Circle from you to myself."

"Quite right, quite right," said Mr. Froyant hastily, "that is the proper way to look at it, Yale. I see that you are not as unintelligent as I thought. Have it your own way," he said. He fingered the notes lovingly, and putting them into a long envelope, handed them, with every evidence of reluctance, to the detective, who slipped the package into his pocket.

"I suppose there is no news of Brabazon? The rascal has robbed me of over two thousand pounds, which I foolishly invested in one of Marl's rotten concerns."

"Did you know anything about Marl?" asked the detective, opening the door.—

"I only know that he was a blackguard."

"Did you know anything that isn't as well known?" asked Yale patiently. "His beginnings, where he came from?"

"He came from France, I believe," said Froyant. "I know very little about him. In fact, it was James Beardmore who introduced me. There was some story about his having been concerned in land swindles in France, and of having been imprisoned there, but I never take much notice of gossip. He was useful to me, and I made quite a considerable sum out of most of my investments with him."

The other smiled. In those circumstances, he thought, the miser might very well forgive the erring Marl for his later losses.

When he got back to his office he found Parr waiting, with Jack Beardmore. He had not expected a visit from the younger man, and guessed that the real attraction was Thalia Drummond, for whose absence he tactfully apologised.

"I've sent Miss Drummond home. Parr," he said. "I don't want a girl mixed up in the business of this afternoon. There may be a little rough-and-tumble work." He looked keenly at Jack Beardmore. "For which I hope you are prepared."

"I shall be disappointed if there isn't," said Jack cheerfully.

"What is your plan?" asked Parr.

"I am going into my room a few minutes before the messenger is due to arrive. I shall have both doors locked, that into the passage and that into this outer office. In the case of this door, I will leave the key on your side and ask you to lock me in. My object, of course, is to prevent a surprise. As soon as you hear a knock, and hear me rise and go to the door and unlock it, you will know that the visitor has arrived, and when the door closes again, I want you to station yourself outside in the corridor."

Parr nodded. "That seems simple," he said. He walked to the window, looked out, and waved a handkerchief, and Yale smiled approvingly.

"I see you have taken the necessary precautions. How many men have you?"

"I think there are eighty," said Mr, Parr calmly, "and they will practically surround the place."

Yale nodded. "We have to remember," he said, "that the Crimson Circle may send a very ordinary district messenger, in which case, of course, he must be followed. I am determined that the money shall pass into the hands of the chief of the Crimson Circle himself—that is an essential."

"I quite agree," said Parr, "but I have an idea that the gentleman, or whoever he is, will not come himself. May I look at your office?"

He walked in and inspected the room. It was lighted by one window. In a corner was a cupboard, the door of which he opened. It was empty save for a hanging coat. "If you don't mind," Inspector Parr was almost humble, "I want you to stay in the outer office. Thank you, I'll close the door on you. I get rattled if I am overlooked." Laughingly Yale walked from the office, and Mr. Parr closed the door on him. He opened the second door, and looked out into the corridor. Presently they heard him close that also.

"You can come in," he said, "I've seen all I want."

The room was simply but comfortably furnished. There was a wide fireplace, in which, however, no fire burnt, although the day was chilly. "I don't expect him to get up the chimney," said Yale, humorously, as he noticed the detective's inspection, "I never have a fire in this office; I'm one of those hot-blooded mortals who are never really cold."

Jack, a fascinated observer of the search, picked up the deadly little pistol that lay on the detective's table, and examined it cautiously.

"Be careful, that trigger is a little sensitive," said Yale.

He took from his pocket the envelope containing the notes, and laid it by the side of the weapon. Then he looked at his watch.

"Now I think that to be on the safe side we should go to the other office, and lock the door," he said, He accompanied his words by locking the door into the corridor.

"It is rather thrilling," whispered Jack. He felt that a whisper was the fitting tone for that exciting moment.

"I hope it won't be too thrilling," said Yale. They went to the outer office, and turned the key on him, and sat down—Jack unconsciously on Thalia Drummond's chair, a fact which he realised with a start.

Was she of the Crimson Circle, he wondered? Parr had hinted as much. Jack set his teeth; he could not, and would not believe even the evidence of his own eyes, and his own common sense. So far from her influence waning, it was gathering strength. She was a being apart, and if she was guilty—He looked up, and saw Parr's eyes fixed upon him. "I don't pretend to be psychometrical," said the detective slowly, "but I've an idea you're thinking about Thalia Drummond."

"I was," admitted the young man. "Mr. Parr, do you think she is really as bad as she appears to be?"

"Do you mean, do I think that she stole Froyant's Buddha, because if that's what you mean, it is not a question of thinking. I am certain."

Jack was silent. He could never hope to convince this stolid man of the girl's innocence and anyway it was madness, he recognised, to think of her as innocent when she had confessed her fault.

"You had better keep quiet in there." It was Yale's voice, and Parr grunted a reply.

Thereafter they sat in dead silence. They heard him moving about the room, then he too was quiet, for the hour was approaching. Inspector Parr pulled his watch from his pocket and laid it on the table; the hands pointed to halt-past three. It was now that the messenger was due and he sat, his head strained forward, listening, but there was no sound of attack.

Presently there was a noise in Yale's room, a queer bumping noise as though Yale had sat down heavily.

Parr jumped to his feet.

"What was that?"

"It is all right," said Yale's voice, "I stumbled over something. Be quiet."

They sat for another five minutes, and then Parr called. "Are you all right, Yale?" There was no answer. "Yale!" he called more loudly. "Do you hear me?"

There was no reply and springing to the door he snapped the lock, and rushed into the room, Jack at his heels.

What he saw might have paralysed even a more experienced officer than Inspector Parr.

Stretched upon the ground, his wrists fastened with handcuffs, his ankles strapped, and a towel over his face lay the prostrate figure of Derrick Yale. The window was open, and there was a strong scent of ether and chloroform. The package of money which had laid upon the table had disappeared. Three seconds later, an aged postman left the hall of the building, carrying his letter-bag on his shoulder, and the police who were watching the house, let him pass without question.

CHAPTER XXIII

THE WOMAN IN THE CUPBOARD

PARR bent down, and snatched the saturated towel from the detective's face, and he opened his eyes, and stared around.

"What is it?" he asked thickly, but the inspector was busy unscrewing the handcuffs. Presently he threw them clanking to the floor, and lifted the man to his feet, as Jack, with trembling fingers, unbuckled the straps about Yale's legs.

They led him to his chair, and he fell heavily into its depths, passing his hand across his forehead.

"What happened?" he asked.

"That's what I'd like to know," said Parr. "Which way did they go?"

The other shook his head.

"I don't know, I can't remember," he said. "Is the door locked?"

Jack ran to the door. The key was turned from the inside. He could not have gone that way, but the window was open. That was the first thing Parr had seen when he entered the room.

He ran to the window, and looked out. There was a sheer fall of eighty feet, and no sign of a ladder or of any means by which Yale's assailant could have escaped.

"I don't know what happened," said Yale, when he had partially recovered. "I was sitting in this chair when suddenly a cloth was pulled across my face, and two powerful hands gripped me with a strength which I shouldn't have thought possible in any human being. Before I could struggle or cry out I must have lost consciousness."

"Did you hear my call?" asked Parr.

The other man shook his head. "But, Mr. Yale, we heard a noise and Mr. Parr asked if you were all right. You replied that you had only stumbled."

"It was not me," said Yale. "I remember nothing from the moment the cloth was put on my face until the moment you found me here."

Inspector Parr was at the window. He pulled down the sash, and he pushed it up again, and then he looked on the window-sill, and when he turned there was a large smile on his face.

"That is the cleverest thing I've ever seen," he said.

Something of Jack's old antipathy to the stout detective returned.

"I don't think it is particularly clever. They've half-killed Yale, and they've got away," he said.

"I said it was clever, and it was clever," said Mr. Parr stolidly, "and now I think I'll go down, and interview the officers I left on duty in the hall."

But the watching officers had nothing to say. "Nobody had entered or left the building except the postman.

"Except the postman, eh?" said Parr thoughtfully. "Why, of course, the postman! All right, sergeant, you can dismiss your men."

He went up in the elevator and rejoined Vale.

"The money's gone all right," he said. "I don't know what we can do except report the matter to head-quarters."

Yale was now nearly his normal self, and sat at his desk with his head resting on his hands. "Well, I'm the culprit this time," he said, "and they can't blame you, Parr. I'm still trying to puzzle out how they got into that window, and how they reached me without making a sound."

"Was your back to the window?"

Yale nodded. "I never dreamt of the window. I sat so that I could see both doors."

"Your back was also to the fireplace?"

"They couldn't have come that way," said the other, shaking his head. "No, this is the supreme mystery of my career; more astounding than the identity of the Crimson Circle," he got up slowly, "I must report this to old man Froyant, and you had better come along and lend me your moral support," he said. "He will be furious."

They left the office together, Yale locking both doors and slipping the key into his pocket.

To say that Mr. Froyant was furious is to employ a very mild expression to describe his hectic frenzy.

"You told me, you practically promised me," he stormed, "that the money would come back to me, and now you have come with a cock-and-bull story of being drugged. It is monstrous! Where were you, Parr?"

"I was on the premises," said Mr. Parr, "and the story Mr. Yale has told is correct."

Suddenly Froyant's rage died down, so suddenly that the calmness of his voice was almost startling after its previous rancour.

"All right," he said, "nothing can be done. The Crimson Circle have had their money, and that is the end of it. I'm much obliged to you, Yale. Please send your bill to me."

And with these brusque instructions, he sent them to rejoin Jack, who was waiting in the street outside.

"Well, that beats the band," said Parr. "I thought at one time he was going to have a fit, and then did you notice how his manner changed?"

Yale nodded slowly. At the moment of Froyant's change of manner a great idea was formed in his mind, a tremendous and startling doubt that was almost paralysing.

"And now," said Parr good-humouredly, "as I have given you moral support, perhaps you will extend the same service to me. At police head-quarters I am not so much persona grata as you. Come along and see the Commissioner and tell him what happened."

Derrick Yale's office was silent and deserted. Ten minutes had passed since the drone of the elevator announced the departure of the three men. The silence was broken by a click, and slowly the doors in the big cupboard in the corner of Derrick Yale's office were pushed open and Thalia Drummond came out. She closed the doors behind her and stood for a while contemplating the room, deep in thought. From her pocket she took a key, opened the door and, passing into the corridor, locked the door behind her.

She did not ring for the elevator. At the farther end of the passage was a flight of narrow stairs which communicated with the caretaker's room, on the top floor, and which were used only by him. Down these she went. At the bottom was a door leading into the courtyard of a building. This, too, she unlocked and soon after had joined the throng of homeward bound clerks that thronged the pavement at this hour.

CHAPTER XXIV

£10,000 REWARD

'The Associated Merchants Bank are authorised to offer a reward of ten thousand pounds for information which will lead to the arrest and conviction of the leader of what is known as the Crimson Circle Gang. In conjunction with this reward the Secretary of State promises a free pardon to any member of the gang, other than one actually guilty of wilful murder, providing that the said member will furnish the information and evidence requisite to the conviction of the man or woman known as the Crimson Circle.'

On every hoarding, in every post office window, on every police station board, the announcement flared in blood-red print.

Derrick Yale, on his way to his office, saw the announcement and read it and passed on, wondering what effect this would have upon the minor members of the gang he had been engaged to hunt.

Thalia Drummond read it from the top of a bus, when that vehicle had pulled up close to a hoarding, to take on a passenger, and she smiled to herself. But the most remarkable effect of the poster was upon Harvey Froyant. It brought a colour to his face and a light to his eye which made him almost youthful. He, too, was on his way to the office when he read the announcement, but hurried back to his house, and took from a drawer in his study a long list.

They were the numbers of the banknotes which the Crimson Circle had taken, and he had compiled them laboriously, almost lovingly.

With his own hands he now made another copy, a work that occupied him until late in the morning. When he had finished he wrote a letter, and enclosing the new list of notes, he addressed it, posting the letter himself, to a firm of lawyers which he knew specialised in the tracing of lost and stolen property.

Heggitts' had rendered him good service before, and the next morning brought a representative of the firm, Mr. James Heggitt, the senior partner, a widened little man with a chronic sniff.

The name of Heggitt was not one which was universally respected, nor did lawyers, when they met, speak of it with affection or regard. And yet it was one of the most prosperous firms of lawyers in the city. The majority of its clients were on or over the border-line which separates the lawful from the unlawful, but to the law-abiding also it was very useful, and was frequently consulted by more eminent firms whose clients wished to recover valuable goods which had been taken by the light-fingered gentry. In some mysterious way Heggitts' could always place their finger upon a "gentleman" who had "heard" of the property which was lost, and, in the majority of cases, the missing article was restored.

"I got your note, Mr. Froyant," said the little lawyer, "and I can tell you now that none of these notes are likely to go through the usual channels." He paused and licked his lips, looking past Mr. Froyant. "The biggest 'fence' of all has gone, so I'm not doing him any injustice when I mention the fact."

"Who was that?"

"Brabazon," was the startling reply, and the other stared at him in astonishment.

"You don't mean Brabazon of Brabazon's Bank?"

"Yes, I do," said Heggitt, nodding. "I should say he did a bigger business in stolen money than any other man in London. You sec, it could pass through his bank without anybody being the wiser, and as he did a lot of business abroad and was constantly changing and re-changing money for export, he got away with it. We knew who was fencing it. At least, when I say we knew," he corrected himself, "we had a shrewd suspicion. As officers of the court, we should, of course, have notified the authorities had we been certain. I thought it better to call to explain to you that it is going to be a very difficult job to trace this money. Most stolen notes are passed on race-courses, but quite a considerable number find their way abroad, where it is a much simpler matter to change them, and where they are ever so much more difficult to trace. You say it was the Crimson Circle who did it?"

"Do you know them?" asked Froyant quickly.

The lawyer shook his head. "I have never had any dealings with them at all," he said, "but, of course, I knew about them, and enough to know that they are clever people. It is likely that this man Brabazon has been doing their work, consciously or unconsciously. In that case they might find a difficulty in disposing of the stuff, for a banknote 'fence' is one of the hardest to find. What am I to do when I track one of these notes and have discovered the person who passed it?"

"I want you to notify me at once," said Froyant, "and nobody else. You understand that this is a matter on which my life may hang, and if by any chance the Crimson Circle get to know that I am trying to recover the money it will be a very serious thing for me."

The lawyer agreed. The Crimson Circle apparently interested him, for he lingered, and skillfully plied his employer with questions without Mr. Froyant realising that he was being pumped.

"They are something new in criminals," he said. "In Italy, where the Black Hand thrives, the demand for money, followed by a threat of death, is quite a common occurrence, but I should not have thought it possible in this country. The most amazing thing of all is that the Crimson Circle holds together. I should imagine," he said thoughtfully, "that there is only one man in it, and that he employs a very considerable number of people unknown to one another and each having his particular job to perform. Otherwise he would have been betrayed a long time ago. It is only the fact that the people serving him do not know him that makes it possible for him to carry on,"

He took up his hat. "By the way, did you know Felix Marl? A client of ours is under charge of burgling his house. Mr. Barnet. You may not have heard of him."

Mr. Froyant had not heard of 'Flush' Barnet, but he knew Marl, and Marl interested him almost as much as the Crimson Circle interested the lawyer. "I knew Marl. Why do you ask?"

The lawyer smiled. "A strange character," he said. "A remarkable character in many ways. He was a member of the gang engaged in frauds on French banks. I suppose you didn't know that? His lawyer came to see me to-day. Apparently a Mrs. Marl has turned up to claim his property, and she has told the whole story. He and a man named Lightman made a fortune in France until they were caught. Marl would have been sent to the guillotine, only he turned State's evidence. Lightman, I believe, went to the knife."

"What a charming man Mr. Marl must have been!" said Mr. Froyant ironically.

The little lawyer smiled. "What charming people we all are when our lives are laid bare!" he said, and Mr. Froyant resented the implied censure, for it was his boast that his life was a book. He might have added in truth a bank-book.

So Brabazon was a dealer in stolen notes and Marl a convicted murderer! Mr. Froyant wondered how Marl managed to escape from his term of imprisonment, which must have been a severe one, and he inwardly rejoiced that his business relationships with the deceased had not ended even more disastrously than they had.

He dressed and went to his club to dine, and his car was running into Pall Mall when a hoarding poster showed under the light of a lamp and reminded him of the unpleasant fact that he was a fifty-thousand pounds poorer man that night than he had been in the morning.

"Ten thousand reward!" he muttered. "Bah! Who is going to turn King's evidence? I don't suppose even Brabazon would dare."

But he did not know Brabazon.

CHAPTER XXV

THE TENANT OF RIVER HOUSE

MR. BRABAZON sat in a chill upper room of River House, eating slowly a large portion of bread and cheese. He wore the dress suit he was wearing when the warning came to him, and he was a ludicrous figure in the smartly-fitting, but now soiled and dusty garb. His white shirt was grey with the grime of the house, he was collarless, and his general air of dissipation was heightened by the stubbly beard that decorated his face.

He finished his repast, opened the window carefully and threw out the remnants of bread, and passing through the trap-door, he descended the ladder and made his way to the big kitchen at the back of the house. He had neither soap nor towel, but he made some attempt to wash himself without their aid, utilising one of the two handkerchiefs he had brought with him to the house in his flight. With the exception of the clothes he stood up in, an overcoat and the soft felt hat he had seized when he made his escape, he was quite unequipped for this undesirable adventure.

The provisions which the mystery man had brought the night after he had reached his hiding place were almost exhausted (he had spent twenty-four hours without any food whatever, but in his agitation had not realised the fact until the stranger arrived carrying a basket of foodstuffs). As to his nerves, they were almost gone. A week spent in that hovel without communion with man, with the knowledge that the police were searching for him, and that a long term of imprisonment would automatically follow his capture, had played havoc with his placid features, and to the solitude had been added the terror of a search.

He had shrunk in a corner behind a door which opened to the inner room leading to the garret whilst the detective had explored the room. The memory of Derrick Yale's visit was a nightmare.

He settled himself down in the old chair that he had found in the house, to spend yet another night. The man whose warning had sent him flying to cover must come soon, and must bring more food.

Brabazon was dozing when he heard the sound of a key put into the lock below and jumped up. He tiptoed carefully to the trap-door and lifted it and then he heard the booming voice of the stranger.

"Come down," it said, and he obeyed.

The previous interview had been in the passage where the darkness seemed thicker than anywhere else in the house. He had accustomed himself to the darkness and walked down the rickety stairs without mishap.

"Stay where you are," said the voice. "I have brought you some food and clothing. You will find everything you need. You had better shave yourself and make yourself presentable."

"Where am I going?" asked Brabazon.

"I have taken a berth for you on a steamer leaving Victoria Dock to-morrow for New Zealand. You will find your passport papers and ticket inm the grip. Now listen. You are to leave your moustache, or what there is of it unshaven, and shave your eyebrows. They are the most conspicuous features of your face,"

Brabazon wondered when this man had seen him. Mechanically his hand stole up to his shaggy eyebrows and mentally he agreed with the mysterious visitor.

"I have not brought you any money," the voice went on. "You have sixty thousand which you stole from Marl—you closed his account, forging his name to a cheque, believing that I would settle with him—as I did."

"Who are you?" asked Brabazon.

"I am the Crimson Circle," was the reply. "Why do you ask that question? You have met me before."

"Yes, of course," Brabazon muttered. "I think this place is driving me mad. When may I leave this house?"

"You may leave to-morrow. Wait until nightfall. Your ship leaves on the following morning, but you can get on board to-morrow night."

"But they will be watching the ship," pleaded Brabazon. "Don't you think it is too dangerous?"

"There is no danger for you," was the reply. "Give me your money."

"My money?" gasped the banker, turning pale.

"Give me your money." There was an ominous note in the voice that spoke in the darkness, and tremblingly Brabazon obeyed. Two large packets of money passed into the gloved hand of the visitor, and then:

"Here, take this."

"This" was a thinner wad of notes, and the sensitive fingers of the banker told him that they were new.

"You can change them when you get abroad," said the man.

"Couldn't I leave to-night?" Brabazon's teeth were chattering now. "This place gives me the horrors." The Crimson Circle was evidently thinking, for it was some time before he spoke.

"If you wish," he said, "but remember you are taking a risk. Now go upstairs." The order was sharp and peremptory, and meekly Brabazon obeyed.

He heard the door close, and peering through the dusty windows, he saw the dark shadow stalk along the path and disappear into the darkness. Presently he heard the gate click. The man was gone.

Brabazon groped for the bag which the other had left and, finding it, carried it to the kitchen. Here he could show a light without fear of detection, and he lit one of the scraps of candle he had discovered in his search of the house during the week.

The stranger had not exaggerated when he said that the bag contained all that Brabazon required. But the banker's first thought was to examine the money which the other had put into his hand. They were notes of all series and all numbers. His own had been in a series, and yet they were new. He looked at them curiously. He knew that new bank-notes were not usually issued higgledy-piggledy, and then he guessed the reason. The Crimson Circle had blackmailed somebody and had asked that the notes should not be numbered consecutively. He put the money down and began to change.

It was a very smart Brabazon who stepped cautiously through the gates carrying his bag an hour later, and yet so remarkable was the change which the shaved eyebrows had made, that when, at eleven o'clock that night, he passed one of the many detective officers who were looking for him, he was unrecognised.

He had engaged a room in a small hotel near Euston Station, and went to bed. It was the first night of untroubled sleep he had enjoyed for over a week.

The next day he spent in his room, not caring to trust himself abroad in daylight, but in the evening, after a solitary meal served in his sitting-room, he went out to take the air. He was gaining in confidence, and was now satisfied that he could pass the scrutiny of the ship detective. He chose the less frequented streets and was passing near the Museum when he saw a bill newly pasted on the hoarding, and stopped to read it.

As he read, an idea took shape. Ten thousand pounds and a free pardon! It was by no means sure that he would escape in the morning; more likely was it that he would be detected, and at best what would his life be? The life of a hunted dog, for which even his money would not compensate him. Ten thousand pounds and freedom! And nobody knew about the money that he had tricked from Felix Marl's estate. He would put that in a safe deposit in the morning, go straight to police head-quarters with information which he felt sure must lead to the Crimson Circle's undoing.

"I'll do it," he said aloud.

"I think you're very wise."

The voice was at his elbow and he swung round.

A little, stocky man had walked noiselessly behind him in his rubber-soled shoes, and Brabazon recognised him instantly.

"Inspector Parr," he gasped. "That's right," said the inspector. "Now, Mr. Brabazon, will you come a little walk with me, or are you going to make trouble?" As they went into the police-station, a woman came out, and the pallid Brabazon failed to recognise his former clerk. He stood in the steel pen whilst the story of his iniquities was told in the cold, official language of the warrant.

"You can save yourself a lot of trouble, Mr. Brabazon," said Inspector Parr, "by telling me the truth. I know where you are staying—at Bright's Hotel in the Euston Road. You arrived there late last night and your passage is booked in the name of Thomson to New Zealand by the Icinga, which is due to leave Victoria Dock to-morrow morning."

"Good God!" said the startled Brabazon. "How did you know that?"

But here Inspector Parr did not inform him.

Brabazon did not intend lying. He told everything he knew. All that had happened from the moment he was called by telephone and told to make a get-away, until he was arrested.

"So you were in the house all the time?" said the inspector thoughtfully. "How did you come to escape Mr. Yale's search?"

"Oh, was it Yale?" said Brabazon. "I thought it was you. There was an inner room—just a little storehouse, I think it was in the old times—I got behind the door and hid. He came almost to the door. I nearly died with fright."

"So Yale was right again. You were there!" said the inspector speaking half to himself. "Now, what are you going to do about it, Brabazon?"

"I'm going to tell you all I know about the Crimson Circle, and I think I can give you information which will lead to his arrest. But you'll have to be smart."

He was recovering something of his old pomposity. Parr observed.

"I told you that he exchanged my notes for his, and his notes for mine. I'm sure he did that because he was afraid of the numbers being taken, but my notes were in a series—series E. 19, and I can give you the number of every one of them," he went on easily. "He wouldn't change the stuff he got."

"That was Froyant's money, I think," said the inspector. "Yes, go on."

"He dare not change that, but he will change mine. Don't you see what a chance this gives to you?"

The inspector was a little sceptical. Nevertheless, after Brabazon had been locked in the cell, he called up Froyant on the 'phone and told him as much of what had happened as was necessary for him to know.

"You've got the money?" said Froyant eagerly. "Come up to the house at once."

"I'll bring it up to the house with pleasure," replied Parr, "but I feel I ought to warn you that this is not your money, although it is the actual cash that was transferred by you to the Crimson Circle."

Later on, in Mr. Froyant's presence, he explained the situation. That spare man made no attempt to hide his disappointment, for he seemed to think that in whatever circumstances the money was recovered, he was entitled to claim. After a while Inspector Parr got him into a more reasonable frame of mind. Froyant was talking quite calmly on the matter, when he suddenly broke off with the question:

"Have you the numbers of the notes which Brabazon handed to him?"

"They are easy to remember," said Parr, "they belong to a series," and he recited the numbers, Mr. Froyant making a rapid note on his desk-pad.

CHAPTER XXVI

THE BOTTLE OF CHLOROFORM

THALIA DRUMMOND was writing a letter when her visitor arrived, and of the many people whom Thalia expected to call, Millie Macroy was the last. The girl looked ill and tired, but she was not so far from human that she could not stand and admire the dainty drawing-room into which Thalia showed her, her servant having gone home for the night.

"Why this is a palace, kid," she said, and regarded Thalia with reluctant admiration. "You know how to do it all right, better than poor 'Flush'."

"And how is the elegant 'Flush'?" asked Thalia coolly.

Millie Macroy's face darkened. "See here," she said roughly, "I don't want any kind of talk about 'Flush' in that tone, do you understand? He is where you ought to be. You were in it as well as him."

"Don't be silly. Take off your hat and sit down. Why, it's like old times seeing you, Macroy."

The girl grumbled something under her breath, but accepted the invitation.

"It is about 'Flush' I want to see you," she said. "There's some talk of framing a murder charge against him, but you know he didn't commit any murder."

"I know? Why should I know?" asked Thalia. "I didn't even know that he was in the house until I read the newspapers in the morning—how wonderfully clever they are on the Press to get news so red-hot."

Milly Macroy had not come to discuss the enterprise of the Press. She drove straight into her subject, which was, as Thalia had expected, 'Flush' Barnet and his immediate prospects.

"Drummond, I'm not going to quarrel with you," she said.

"I'm glad of that," said Thalia. "I can't exactly see what there is to quarrel about, anyway."

"That may or may not be," said Miss Macroy, ironically. "The point is, what are you going to do for 'Flush'? You know all these swells, and you're working for that swine Yale," she almost hissed. "It was Yale who put Parr up to the Marisburg Place job; Parr hadn't got brains enough to think it out for himself. Were you working with Yale all the time?"

"Don't make me laugh," said Thalia scornfully. "It's certainly true I am working for Yale, if writing his letters and tidying his desk is work. But what swells are you talking about? And what can I do for 'Flush' Barnet?"

"You can go to Inspector Parr and tell him the old, old story," said Macroy. "I've got it all worked out; you can say that 'Flush' was sweet on you, saw you go into the house and followed, and couldn't get out."

"What about my young reputation?" asked the girl coolly. "No, Milly Macroy, you've got to think up something prettier and, anyway, I don't think they're making a charge for murder against him, from what Derrick Yale said this morning."

She rose and walked slowly across the room, her hands clasped behind her.

"Besides, what interest have I in your young man? Why should I take the trouble of speaking for him?"

"I'll tell you why." Miss Macroy rose, her hands on her hips, and glared at the girl. "Because when the Brabazon case comes on, there's nothing to prevent me going into the box and saying a few plain words about what you did in the way of quick money-getting when you were Brab's secretary. Ah! That's made you jump, miss!"

"When the Brabazon case comes on!" said the girl slowly. "Why? Have they caught Brabazon?"

"They pinched him to-night," answered the girl triumphantly. "Parr did it: I was up at the police station making inquiries about some money that 'Flush' left over for me, when they brought him in."

"Brabazon a prisoner," said Thalia slowly. "Poor old Brab!"

Macroy was watching her through her half-closed lids. She had never liked Thalia Drummond, and now she hated her. She feared her too, for there was something sinister in her very coolness. Presently Thalia spoke. "I'll do what I can for 'Flush' Barnet," she said. "Not because I'm scared of your going into the box—that's the part of the police court where you'll be least at home, Macroy—but because the poor little wretch was innocent of the murder."

Miss Macroy swallowed something at this description of her lover.

"I'll talk to Yale in the morning. I can't be sure it will do any good, but I'll get a heart-to-heart talk with him if he gives me a chance."

"Thank you," said Miss Macroy, a little more graciously, and proceeded to admire the flat in conventional language. Thalia showed her from room to room.

"What's this place?"

"The kitchen," said Thalia, but made no attempt to open the door. The girl looked at her suspiciously, "Have you got a friend?" she asked, and before Thalia could stop her she had opened the door and walked in.

The kitchen was a small one and empty. The electric light was burning, which suggested to Miss Macroy that the girl had left the kitchen to answer her knock.

Thalia could have smiled at the obvious disappointment on Milly Macroy's face, but her inclination to amusement departed as Macroy walked to the sink and picked up a bottle.

"What is this?" said she, and read the label. It was half-filled with a colourless liquid, and Miss Macroy did not attempt to take out the stopper. The label told her all she wanted to know.

"'Chloroform and Ether'," she read, looking at the girl. "Why have you been using chloroform?" Only for a second was Thalia taken aback, and then she laughed.

"Well, do you know, Milly Macroy," she drawled, "when I think of poor 'Flush' Barnet in Brixton Gaol, I have to sniff something to put him out of my mind." Macroy banged down the bottle on the table with a snort. "You're a bad lot, Thalia Drummond, and one of these days they'll be waking you at eight o'clock, and ask you if you have any message for your friends."

"And I shall reply," said Thalia sweetly, "bury me next to 'Flush' Barnet, the eminent crook."

Miss Milly Macroy did not think of a suitable retort until she was in the Marylebone Road, and then it came to her with annoying force that, for all her interview, Thalia Drummond had promised nothing.

CHAPTER XXVII

MR. PARR'S MOTHER

JACK BEARDMORE had heard of Brabazon's arrest, and went straight to police head-quarters to see Mr. Parr. He found that excellent gentleman had gone home. "If it is important, Mr. Beardmore," said the police clerk on duty, "you will find him at home in his house at Stamford Avenue."

Beyond his natural interest in the Crimson Circle and all that pertained thereto. Jack had no particular wish to see the inspector, and Derrick Yale had telephoned all that was known or could be told.

"Parr thinks this arrest may have an important development," he said. "No, I haven't seen Brabazon, but I accompany Parr to-morrow morning when he visits him."

Yale, too, was apparently un-get-at-able; he had hinted that he had a theatre party that night, and Jack bent his steps homeward. He had sent his car away, for he felt he needed exercise to dissipate his energies, and as he crossed the gloomy park, taking a short cut to his house, he found himself wondering what sort of a home life a man like Parr could have. He had never spoken about his family, and his mode of living outside of the police head-quarters was almost as much of a mystery as that which he was trying to unravel.

Where was Stamford Avenue, he wondered. He had reached a deserted spot of the park, when he thought he heard footsteps behind him, and turned his head. He was not a nervous type, and ordinarily the sound of somebody walking in his rear would not have interested him sufficiently to make him turn. The path here skirted a dense thicket of rhododendrons. There was nobody in sight. Jack went on, quickening his pace.

He heard no more footsteps, but looking round he thought he saw a man walking on the grass by the side of the path. As Jack stopped he too halted. He was doubtful as to what he should do. To challenge the man might put him into an absurd position; there was no reason in the world why any good citizen should not walk in the park at night, or, for the matter of that, why they should not walk behind him anywhere at a respectable distance.

And then ahead of him he made out a slowly strolling figure, and heard the unmistakable "beat walk" of a policeman.

To his own amazement he felt relieved, and when he looked round, the figure that had followed him had disappeared. He tried to reconstruct his impression; whoever his tracker had been, he was smally made. At first Jack had thought it was a boy; perhaps some poor park beggar who was mustering up courage to approach him for the price of a night's bed. It seemed absurd that he was glad to be out of the park, and to step into the well-lighted street, but it was the case.

He made an inquiry of a policeman.

"Stamford Avenue, sir? That bus you see over there will take you, or you can get there in a taxi in ten minutes."

Jack stood for a long time before he called the taxi-cab. Mr. Parr would rightly resent this intrusion into his domestic privacy, and really he had no excuse to offer. But making up his mind of a sudden, he called a cab, and in a very short time was experiencing exactly the same doubts and misgivings before the door of Inspector Parrs' maisonette.

It was Parr himself who opened the door. His face was naturally free from expression, and he neither showed surprise nor annoyance at the arrival of his late visitor.

"Come in, Mr. Beardmore," he said. "I have just arrived, and am having supper. I suppose you've had your evening meal a long time ago."

"Don't let me interrupt you, Mr. Parr, only I was rather interested to hear that you had caught Brabazon, and I thought I'd come along."

The inspector was showing him into the dining-room, when suddenly he stopped.

"Good Lord!" he said. Jack could only wonder what had startled him. "Do you mind waiting here?" For the first time since Jack had known the police officer, Parr was embarrassed. "I must first tell an old aunt of mine who is staying here who you are," he said. "She's not used to visitors. I'm a widower, you know, and my aunt keeps house for me." He entered the dining-room hurriedly, closing the door behind him, and Jack felt something of his host's embarrassment.

A minute, two minutes passed. He heard a hurried movement in the room, and Parr opened the door. "Come in, sir." His red face was even a deeper red. "Sit you down, and please forgive me for keeping you waiting."

The room in which he found himself was well and tastefully furnished. Jack was annoyed with himself for expecting anything else.

Mr. Parr's aunt was a faded lady with an absent manner, and she seemed to cause Mr. Parr a considerable amount of anxiety. He scarcely took his eyes from her as she moved about the room, and she hardly spoke before he jumped in to interrupt her, always politely, but always very definitely.

The inspector's supper was set upon a tray; he had just about finished when Jack had knocked at the door.

"I hope you'll excuse our untidiness, Mr.—er—"

"Beardmore," said Jack.

"She'll never remember it," murmured the inspector.

"I can't keep the place as mother kept it," she said.

"Of course not, of course not, auntie," said Mr. Parr hurriedly. "A little absent," he murmured. "Now what did you want to know, Mr. Beardmore?"

Jack laughingly excused himself for his call. "The Crimson Circle is such a complicated business that I suspect every new agent to be the central figure," he said. "Do you think that the arrest of Brabazon is going to help us?"

"I don't know," replied Parr slowly. "There is just a chance that Brabazon will be a very big help indeed. By the way, I've put one of my own men to look after him, and I have given instructions that the jailer is not to go into the cell under any circumstances."

"You're thinking of Sibly, the sailor, who was poisoned?"

Parr nodded. "Don't you think, Mr. Beardmore, that that was one of the greatest mysteries of all the mysterious Crimson Circle murders?" He asked this question very soberly, but there was a little glint in his eye which Jack did not fail to notice.

"You're laughing. Why? I think it was mysterious, don't you?"

"Very," said the inspector. "In some respects, and the poisoning of Sibly will, to my mind, be a much more important factor in the eventual capture of the Crimson Circle than is the arrest of our friend Brabazon."

"I wish you wouldn't talk about crime and criminals," said his aunt fretfully; "really, John, you are very trying. It may have suited mother—"

"Yes, of course, auntie; I'm sorry," said Parr hurriedly, and when she had left the room, Jack Beardmore's curiosity got the better of his discretion.

"Mother seems to have been rather a paragon," he smiled, and wondered if he had made a faux pas.

The answering laugh reassured him. "Yes, rather a paragon; she is not staying with us just now."

"Is she your mother, Mr. Parr?"

"No, my grandmother," said Mr. Parr, and Jack looked at him in astonishment.

CHAPTER XXVIII

A SHOT IN THE NIGHT

THE inspector must have been nearly fifty, and he made a rapid calculation as to the age of this wonderful grandmother who took an interest in crime, and kept the house tidy.

"She must be a wonderful old lady," he said, "and I suppose she'd even be interested in the Crimson Circle?"

"Interested!" Mr. Parr laughed. "If mother was on the track of that gang with the same authority as I have, they would be high and dry in Cannon Street police station to-night. As it is," he paused, "they are not."

All the time they were talking Jack was puzzling his head as to why, in spite of its order, the room gave him an impression of untidiness. But he was not left to his own thoughts for very long, for Mr. Parr was in an unusually communicative mood. He even went so far as to tell Jack some of the unpleasant things said to him by the Commissioner.

"Naturally police head-quarters are rather rattled by the continuance of these crimes," he said. "We haven't had anything like this for fifty years. In fact, I don't think since the Ripper murders there has been such an orgy of destruction. It may interest you, too, Mr. Beardmore, to know that the Crimson Circle, whoever he is, is the first real organising criminal we have had to deal with for nearly fifty years. Criminal organisations are loose affairs, and as they depend for their safety upon that sense of honour which every thief is supposed to possess, but which I have never met with, the game doesn't last very long. The Crimson Circle, however, is a man who obviously trusts nobody. He cannot be betrayed because nobody is in a position to betray him. Even the minor members of the gang cannot betray one another, because it is just as clear to me that they do not know one another by name or by sight." He went on to discuss interestingly cases in which he had been concerned, and it was nearly half-past eleven when Jack rose with a further apology.

"I'll take you to the front door; your car is here, isn't it?"

"No," said Jack. "I came by taxi."

"H'm," said the inspector. "I thought I saw a car drawn up in front of the door. We are not a motor-car owning neighbourhood; probably it is a doctor's machine."

He opened the door, and, as he had said, a black car was drawn up at the kerb.

"I seem to have seen that before," said the inspector, and took a step forward. As he did so a pencil of flame leapt from the dark interior of the car; there was a deafening report, and Inspector Parr fell into Jack's arms and slid to the ground. A second later and the car was speeding up the street; it showed no light and vanished round the corner as the doors in the street began to open and to let out the alarmed residents.

A policeman came running along the pavement, and together they lifted the detective and carried him into the dining-room. Happily the aunt had gone to bed, and had apparently heard and noticed nothing.

Inspector Parr opened his eyes and blinked. "That was a nasty one," he said with a wince of pain. He felt gingerly in his waistcoat and brought out a flat piece of lead. "I'm glad he didn't use an automatic," he said, and then, seeing the blank amazement on Jack's face, he grinned.

"The Crimson Circle gentleman is only one of three who wear a bullet-proof waistcoat," he said. "I am the second, and—" he paused, "Thalia Drummond is the third, as I happen to know."

He did not speak again for some time, and then he said to Jack:

"Will you telephone to Derrick Yale? I think he is going to be considerably startled." The prophecy understated the case. Derrick Yale arrived half an hour after the shooting in such haste that his appearance suggested that he had dressed over his pyjama suit. He listened to Parr's story, and then: "I don't want to be uncomplimentary, inspector," he laughed, "but you're the last person in the world I should have thought they would have wanted to shoot."

"Thank you," said Parr, who was gingerly fixing a lint pad over his bruised chest. "I don't mean that as uncomplimentary; I merely mean that such a definite challenge to the police is the last thing in the world I expected them to deliver." He frowned heavily. "I don't understand it," he said as though speaking to himself. "I wonder why she wanted to know. I'm talking about Thalia Drummond. She asked me this morning what was your address," he said. "I understand your name is not even in the telephone book or in the local directory."

"What did you say?"

"I gave her some evasive answer, but I've just remembered that my private address book is accessible, and she could easily have discovered it without troubling to ask me. I wonder she didn't."

Jack gave a weary sigh. "Really, Yale, you're not suggesting that Miss Drummond fired that shot, are you? Because, if you are, it's a ridiculous suggestion. Oh, I know what you're going to say: she's a bad lot and has been guilty of all sorts of miserable little crimes, but that doesn't make her a murderess!"

"You're quite right," replied Yale after a pause. "I'm being unjust to the girl, and it doesn't seem that I'm starting fair if I am sincere in my desire to give her a chance. I wanted to see you to-night, by the way, Parr." He took from his pocket a card and laid it on the table before the inspector. "How does that strike you for nerve?"

"When did you get it?"

"It was waiting in the letter-box for me, but I didn't see it, curiously enough, until I was rushing out to find a taxi to bring me here. Isn't it colossal?"

The card bore a symbol familiar enough to the two men, but at the very sight of that Crimson Circle, Jack shuddered. Within the hoop was written: 'You are serving the losing side. Serve us instead and you shall be rewarded tenfold. Continue your present work, and you die on the fourth of next month.'

"That gives you about ten days," said Parr seriously, and it might have been the pain he had suffered, or excitement, but he seemed suddenly to lose his colour. "Ten days," he muttered.

"Of course, I take not the slightest notice of that threat," said Derrick Yale cheerfully. "I must confess that after my unpleasant experience at the office I almost credit them with supernatural gifts."

"Ten days," repeated the detective. "Have you made any plans? Ordinarily, where would you be on the fourth of next month?"

"It is curious that you should ask that," said Yale, "but I had arranged to go down to Deal for some fishing. A friend of mine has lent me a motor-launch, and I thought of spending the night in the Channel; in fact, I had arranged to go on that day."

"You can make what arrangements you like, but you are not going alone," said Parr emphatically. "And now you can all clear out. Thank your lucky stars that my aunt has not wakened, and that mother isn't here."

The last he said was intended for Jack, and Jack smiled understandingly.

CHAPTER XXIX

THE RED CIRCLE

IT was Harvey Froyant's boast that he trusted nobody completely. He trusted the lawyer up to a point, but his known connection with questionable people would have been alone sufficient to prevent Harvey from trusting implicitly to his agent. Two nights after the shooting of Inspector Parr the little lawyer called on his employer, and he was all a-quiver with excitement. He had traced one of the new series of bank-notes which the Crimson Circle had taken from Brabazon.

"Now, we've got a good line on this, Mr. Froyant, and if we continue in the direction we are going, we can certainly pick up the original changer."

But here Mr. Harvey Froyant was firm. He could not and would not place the case completely in the hands of this man. So far might the knowledgeable firm of Heggitt take him, but he would carry on the rest through another agency. He said so in as many words.

"I'm sorry you won't let me go on with it," said the disappointed Heggitt. "I have undertaken this search personally, and I can assure you that there are only a few steps now between the man we discovered with the money and the man you are looking for."

Harvey Froyant knew that as well as the lawyer. Jack Beardmore had spoken a great truth when he said that this mean man would never be satisfied until he had recovered the money he had lost. It was a goad and an irritation, a source of thought which kept him awake at night and woke him in the morning with a sense of blank despair.

And Harvey was well equipped to carry the investigations to their final stage now that he had the ground clear for him. He had derived his fortune from buying and selling land in every country in the world. Beginning with practically no capital, he had, by personal application to his business, built up a seven figure fortune. And this had not been accomplished by sitting in an office and trusting to subordinates. It had involved considerable travel, restless inquiry and relentless probing into the private circumstances of negotiators, a peculiarity he had shared with James Beardmore, though this he did not know.

He took up his own case with alacrity, and informed neither Yale nor Parr of his intentions.

As Heggitt had said, it was a fairly simple matter to trace the note, for at least three stages. His investigations brought Mr. Froyant successively to a money-changer's in the Strand, a tourist office and finally to a highly respectable bank. And here he was particularly favoured, for it was a branch of one of the banks which conducted his business. For three days he pried and questioned, searched books—which he had no right to search—and slowly but surely he came to a conclusion. He was not, however, satisfied to leave the matter with the discovery of the original passer of the note. Not even the bank manager, who gave him facilities for examining private accounts, and was afterwards reprimanded by his superiors for doing so, knew exactly what object he had, or against whom his investigations were directed.

On the morning of the first day Froyant left hurriedly for France. He spent only two hours in Paris, and the night found him on his way to the south. Toulouse he reached at nine o'clock in the morning; here again luck was with him, for an important official of the city had been an agent of his in a purchase he had made a few years before. Monsieur Brassard offered his guest an emphatic welcome, which Mr. Froyant discounted on the ground that his former agent was under the impression that a new deal and a new commission was in prospect. This seemed to be the case, for he was less enthusiastic when he learnt the object of the visit.

"I do not trouble myself with these matters," he said, shaking his head, "for although I am a lawyer, my dear Mr. Froyant, my practice does not touch the criminal court." He stroked his long beard thoughtfully. "I remember Marl very well indeed—Marl and another man, an Englishman, I think."

"A man named Lightman?"

"Yes, that was the fellow. Good gracious, yes!" He made a grimace of disgust. "Of course, that is common history," he went on. "They were scoundrels, those men. One shot the cashier and the watchman of the Nimes Bank, and there were two murders here in Toulouse with which their names were associated. I remember their names very well—and the terrible incident!" He shook his head.

"What terrible incident?" asked Mr. Froyant curiously.

"It was when Lightman was led to execution. I think our executioners must have been drunk, for the knife did not work; twice, three times it fell, but only just touched his neck. And when the horrified spectators interfered—you know our French people are very emotional—there would have been a riot if they had not taken the prisoner back to gaol. Yes, the Red Circle escaped the knife."

Mr. Froyant, who was sipping a cup of coffee, leapt to his feet, overturning the cup and its contents.

"The what?" he almost shouted.

Mr. Brassard looked at him open-mouthed.

"Why, what is wrong, m'sieur?" he asked, one eye on the damaged carpet.

"The Red Circle! What do you mean?" demanded Froyant, trembling with excitement.

"That was Lightman," nodded Brassard, astonished at the effect his words produced. "It was his public name. But my clerk will know more, for he was interested in the matter, which I was not."

He rang the bell, and an elderly Frenchman came in.

"Do you remember the Red Circle, Jules?"

The aged Jules nodded. "Very well, m'sieur. I was at the execution. What horror!" He raised his two hands in an expressive gesture.

"Why was he called the Red Circle?" demanded Froyant.

"Because of a mark." The man drew his long finger about his neck. "Around his throat, m'sieur, was a red circle; it was the colour of his skin, and it was a legend long before the execution that no knife would ever touch him, for such marks are said to be charmed. I think it was a birth-mark, but I know that on the way to the execution I met a great number of people—my friend Thiep, for example—who were sure that the execution would not take place. If they were as sure that the executioner and his assistants would be drunk," added Jules, "and that they had put up the guillotine in the morning so badly that the knife would not work, I think they would have been more intelligent."

Mr. Froyant was now breathing quickly. Little by little the truth was being revealed, and now he saw the whole thing clearly.

"What happened to the Red Circle?" he asked.

"I do not know," shrugged Jules. "He was sent to one of the island settlements, but Marl was released because he had given evidence for the Republic. I heard some time ago that Lightman had escaped, but I don't know how true that is."

Lightman had escaped, as Froyant had already guessed. He passed that day in a feverish search of all available documents, in a visit to the Public Prosecutor, and he ended a strenuous twelve hours in the bureau of the prison governor, examining photographs.

It may be said that Mr. Harvey Froyant went to bed that night in the Hotel Anglaise with a feeling of complete satisfaction, and with the added pleasure that he had succeeded where the cleverest police had failed. The secret of the Crimson Circle was no longer a secret.

CHAPTER XXX

THE SILENCING OF FROYANT

HARVEY FROYANT'S visit to France had not escaped attention, and both Derrick Yale and Inspector Parr knew that he had gone; so also did the Crimson Circle, if Thalia Drummond's telegram reached its destination.

Curiously enough these telegrams and messages which Thalia was sending was the excuse for Derrick Yale's call at police headquarters, on the very evening that Mr. Froyant was returning triumphantly from France.

Parr, returning to his office, found Yale sitting at the inspector's table, delighting a small but select audience of police officials with an exhibition of his curious power.

His ability in this direction was amazing. From a ring which a police inspector handed him he told the mystified hearer not only his known history but, to his confusion, a little secret history of the man's life.

As Parr came in his assistant gave him a sealed envelope. He glanced at the typewritten address, and then laid it on Yale's outstretched hand. "Tell me who sent that?" he said, and Yale laughed.

"A very small man with an absurd yellow beard; he talks through his nose and keeps a shop."

A slow smile dawned on Parr's face. Yale added: "And that isn't psychometry, because I happen to know it is from Mr. Johnson of Mildred Street." He chuckled at the inspector's blank expression, and when they were alone, explained.

"I happen to know that you discovered the place to which all the Crimson Circle messages were sent. I, on the contrary, have known of its existence for a long time, and every message which has been sent to the Crimson Circle has been read by me. Mr. Johnson told me you were making inquiries, and I asked him to give you a very full explanation in the addressed envelope which you sent to him."

"So you knew it all the time?" asked Parr slowly.

Derrick Yak nodded. "I know that messages intended for the Crimson Circle have been addressed to this little newsagent, and that every afternoon and evening a small boy calls to collect them. It is a humiliating confession to make, but I have never been able to trace the person who picks the boy's pocket."

"Picks his pocket?" repeated Parr, and Yale enjoyed the mystery.

"The boy's instructions are to put the letters in his pocket, and to walk into the crowded High Street. Whilst he is there somebody takes them from his pocket without his being any the wiser."

Inspector Parr sat down on the chair which Yale had vacated, and rubbed his chin.

"You're an amazing fellow," he said. "And what else have you discovered?"

"What I have all along suspected," said Yale, "that Thalia Drummond is in communication with the Crimson Circle and has given him every scrap of information which she has been able to gather."

Parr shook his head. "What are you going to do about that?"

"I told you all along that she would lead us to the Crimson Circle," said Yale quietly, "and sooner or later I am sure my predictions will be justified. It is nearly two months since I induced our friend who keeps a small newsagent's shop to which letters may be addressed, to give me the first look over all letters addressed to Johnson. He wanted a little inducing, because our newsagent is a very honest, straightforward man, but it is my experience, and probably yours, that the mere suggestion that a man is assisting the cause of justice will induce him to commit the most outrageous acts of disloyalty. I took the liberty of suggesting, without stating, that I was a regular police officer. I hope you don't mind."

"There are times when I think you should be a regular police officer," said Parr. "So Thalia Drummond is in communication with the Crimson Circle?"

"I shall continue to employ her, of course," said Yale. "The closer she is to me, the less dangerous she will be."

"Why did Froyant go abroad?" asked Parr.

The other shrugged his shoulders. "He has many business connections abroad, and probably is engaged in a deal. He owns about a third of the vineyards in the Champagne. I suppose you know that?"

The inspector nodded. Then, for some reason or other, a silence fell upon them. Each man was busy with his own thoughts, and Mr. Parr particularly was thinking of Froyant, and wondering why he had gone to Toulouse, "How did you know he had gone to Toulouse?" asked Derrick Yale.

The question was so unexpected, such a startling continuation of his own thoughts, that Parr jumped. "Good heavens!" he said, "can you read a man's mind?"

"Sometimes," said Yale, unsmilingly. "I thought he had gone to Paris."

"He went to Toulouse," said the inspector shortly, and did not explain how he came to know.

Possibly nothing Derrick Yale had ever done, no demonstration he had given of his gifts, had so disconcerted this placid inspector of police as that experiment in thought transference. It alarmed, indeed, frightened him, and he was still shaken in his mind when Harvey Froyant's telephone call came through.

"Is that you, Parr? I want you to come to my house. Bring Yale with you. I have a very important communication to make."

Inspector Parr hung up the receiver deliberately, "Now, what the devil does he know?" he said, speaking to himself, and Derrick

Yale's keen eyes, which had not left the inspector's face all the time he was speaking, shone for a moment with a strange light.

Thalia Drummond had finished her simple dinner and was engaged in the domestic task of darning a stocking. Her undomestic task, which was of greater urgency, was to prevent herself thinking of Jack Beardmore. There were times when the thought of him was an acute agony, and since such moments of quietness and solitude as these were favourable for such meditation, she had just put down her work and turned to something new for distraction, when the door bell rang. It was a district messenger, and he carried in his hand a square parcel that looked like a boot box.

It was addressed to her in pen-printed characters, and she had a little flutter at her heart as she realised from whom it had come. Back in her room she cut the string and opened the box.

On the top lay a letter which she read. It was from the Crimson Circle, and ran:

'You know the way into Froyant's house. There is an entrance from the garden into the bomb-proof shelter beneath his study. Gain admission, taking with you the contents of this box. Wait in the underground room until I give you further instructions.'

She lifted out the contents of the box. The first article was a large gauntlet glove that reached almost to her elbow. It was a man's glove, and left-handed. The only other thing in the box was a long, sharp-pointed knife with a cup-like guard. She handled it carefully, feeling the edge; it was as sharp as a razor. For a long time she sat looking at the weapon and the glove, and then she got up and went to the telephone and gave a number. She waited for a long time, until the operator told her there was no answer.

At nine o'clock, she looked at her watch. It was past eight already, and she had no time to lose. She put the glove and the knife in a big leather hand-bag, wrapped herself in her cloak, and went out.

Half an hour later, Derrick Yale and Mr. Parr ascended the steps of Froyant's residence and were admitted by a servant. The first thing Derrick Yale noticed was that the passage was brilliantly illuminated; all the lights in the hall were on, and even the lamps on the landing above were in full blaze, a curious circumstance, remembering Mr. Harvey Froyant's parsimony. Usually he contented himself with one feeble light in the hall, and any room in the house that was not in use was in darkness.

The library was a room opening from the main hall; the door was wide open, and the visitors saw that the room was as brilliantly lighted as the hall. Harvey Froyant was sitting at his desk, a smile on his tired face, but for all his weariness there was self-satisfaction in every gesture, every note in his voice.

"Well, gentlemen," he said almost jovially, "I'm going to give you a little information which I think will startle and amuse you." He chuckled and rubbed his hands. "I have just called up the Chief Commissioner, Parr," he said, peering up at the stout detective. "In a case like this one wants to be on the safe side. Anything may happen to you two gentlemen after you leave this house, and we cannot have too many people in our secret. Will you take your overcoats off? I am going to tell you a story which may take some time."

At that moment the telephone bell trilled, and they stood watching him as he took down the receiver.

"Yes, yes, colonel," he said. "I have a very important communication to make; may I call you up in a second or two? You will be there? Good." He replaced the instrument. They saw him frown undecidedly, and then: "I think I'll talk to the colonel now, if you don't mind stepping into another room and closing the door. I don't want to anticipate the little sensation which I am creating."

"Certainly," said Parr, and walked from the room.

Derrick Yale hesitated. "Is this communication about the Crimson Circle?"

"I will tell you," said Mr. Froyant. "Just give me five minutes and then you shall have your thrill of sensation." Derrick Yale laughed, and Parr, who had reached the hall, smiled in sympathy.

"It takes a lot to thrill me," said Derrick. He came out of the room, stood for a moment with the door edge in his hand. "And afterwards I think I shall be able to tell you something about our young friend

Drummond," he said. "Oh, I know you're not interested, but this little fact will interest you perhaps as much as the story you are going to tell us."

Parr saw him smile, and guessed that Froyant had growled something uncomplimentary about Thalia Drummond. Derrick Yale closed the door softly. "I wonder what his sensation is, Parr," he mused thoughtfully. "And what the dickens has he to tell your colonel?"

They walked into the front drawing-room, which was equally well lighted.

"This is unusual, isn't it, Steere?" said Derrick Yale, who knew the butler.

"Yes, sir," said the stately man. "Mr. Froyant is not as a rule extravagant in the matter of current. But he told me that he'd want all the lights to-night, and that he was not taking any risks, whatever that might mean. I've never known him to do such a thing. He's got two loaded revolvers in his pocket—that is what strikes me as queer. He hates firearms, does Mr. Froyant, as a rule."

"How do you know he has revolvers?" asked Parr sharply.

"Because I loaded them for him," replied the butler. "I used to be in the Yeomanry, and I understand the use of weapons. One of them is mine."

Derrick Yale whistled and looked at the inspector. "It looks as if he not only knows the Crimson Circle, but he expects a visit," he said. "By the way, have you any men on hand?"

Parr nodded. "There are a couple of detectives in the street; I told them to hang around in case they were wanted," he said. They could not hear Froyant's voice at the telephone, for the house was solidly built, and the walls were thick.

Half an hour passed, and Yale grew impatient.

"Will you ask him if he wants us, Steere?" he said, but the butler shook his head.

"I can't interrupt him, sir. Perhaps one of you gentlemen would go in. We never go in unless we are rung for." Parr was half-way out of the room, and in an instant had flung open the door of Harvey Froyant's study. The lights were blazing, and he had no doubt of what had happened from the second his eyes fell upon the figure huddled back in his chair. Harvey Froyant was dead. The handle of a knife projected from his left breast, a knife with a steel cup-like guard. On the narrow desk was a blood-stained leather gauntlet.

It was the startled cry of Parr that brought Derrick Yale rushing into the room. Parr's face was as white as death as he stared at the tragic figure in the chair, and neither man spoke a word. Then Parr spoke. "Call my men in," he said. "Nobody is to leave this house. Tell the butler to assemble the servants in the kitchen and keep them there."

He took in every detail of the room. Across the big windows which looked on to a square of green at the back of the house, heavy velvet curtains were drawn. He pulled them aside. Behind these were shutters and they were securely fastened.

How had Harvey Froyant been killed?

His desk was opposite the fire-place, and the desk was a narrow Jacobean affair which would have distracted any ordinary man by its lack of width, but it was a favourite of the dead financier.

From which way had the murderer approached him?

From behind? The knife was thrust in a downward direction, and the theory that his assailant came upon him unawares was at least plausible. But why the glove? Inspector Parr handled it gingerly. It was a leather gauntlet, such as a chauffeur uses, and had been well worn.

His next move was to call the Police Commissioner and, as he had suspected, the colonel was waiting for a communication from Harvey Froyant.

"Then he did not telephone to you?"

"No. What has happened?"

Parr told him briefly, and listened unmoved to the almost incoherent fury of his chief at the other end of the wire. Presently he hung up the receiver and went back to the hall, to find his men already posted.

"I am searching every room in the house," he said, He was gone half an hour, and returned to Derrick Yale.

"Well?" asked Yale eagerly.

Parr shook his head. "Nothing," he said. "There is nobody here who has no right to be here."

"How did they get into the room? The hall-way was never empty except when Steere came into the drawing-room."

"There may be a trap in the floor," suggested Yale.

"There are no traps in drawing-room floors in the West End of London," snapped Parr, but a further search had a surprising result. Turning up one corner of the carpet, a small trap-door was discovered, and the butler explained that in the days of the war, when air raids were a nightly occurrence, Mr. Froyant had had a bomb-proof shelter constructed of concrete in a lower wine cellar, ingress to which was gained by means of a flight of stairs leading from his study.

Parr went down the stairs with a lighted candle and discovered himself in a small, square, cell-like room. There was a door, which was locked, but, searching the body of Harvey Froyant, they found a master key. Beyond the first door was a second of steel and this brought them into the open.

The houses in the street shared a common strip of lawn and shrubbery.

"It is quite possible to get into here through the gate at the end of the garden," said Yale, "and I should say that the murderer came this way."

He was flashing his electric lamp along the ground. Suddenly he went down on to the ground and peered. "Here is a recent footprint," he said, "and a woman's!"

Parr looked over his shoulder. "I don't think there is any doubt about that," he said. "It is recent." And then suddenly he stepped back. "My God!" he gasped in awe-stricken tones. "What a devilish plot!"

For it came upon him with a rush that this was the footprint of Thalia Drummond.

CHAPTER XXXI

THALIA ANSWERS A FEW QUESTIONS

DERRICK YALE sat with his head on his hands, reading a newspaper. He had read a dozen that morning, and one by one he had cast them aside to open another.

"Under the eyes of the police," he quoted. "Incompetence at Police Head-quarters." He shook his head. "They are giving our poor friend Parr a bad time in this morning's press," he said as he threw the paper aside, "and yet he was as incapable of preventing that crime as you or I, Miss Drummond."

Thalia Drummond looked a little peaked that morning. There were dark circles about her eyes, and an air of general listlessness which was in contrast to her usual cheerful buoyancy.

"If you're in that game you expect to get kicks, don't you?" she asked coolly. "The police can't have it all their own way."

He looked at her curiously. "You aren't a particular admirer of police methods, are you, Miss Drummond?" he asked.

"Not tremendously," she replied, as she laid a stack of correspondence before him. "You aren't expecting me to get up testimonials to the efficiency of head-quarters, are you?"

He laughed quietly. "You're a strange girl," he said. "Sometimes I think that you were born without compassion. You worked for Froyant, too, didn't you?"

"Yes," she said shortly.

"You lived some time in the house?"

She did not reply, but her grey eyes met his steadily. "I did live some time in the house," she admitted.

"Why do you ask that?"

"I wondered if you knew of the existence of this underground room?" said Derrick Yale carelessly.

"Of course I knew of the room. Poor Mr. Froyant made no secret of his cleverness. He has told me a dozen times how much it cost," she added with a faint smile.

He cogitated a moment. "Where were the keys usually kept that opened the door of the bomb-proof room?"

"In Mr. Froyant's desk. Are you suggesting that I have had access to them, or that I was concerned in last night's murder?"

He laughed. "I am not suggesting anything," he said, "I am merely inquiring, and as you seem to know a great deal more about the house than most of the people who live in it, my curiosity is natural. Would it be possible, do you think, to push up that trap without making a noise?"

"Quite," she said. "The trap-door works on counterbalances. Are you going to answer any of those letters?"

He pushed the pile of letters aside. "What were you doing last light, Miss Drummond?"

This time his method was more direct. "I spent my evening at home," she said. Her hands went behind her, and that curious rigidity which he had noticed before stiffened her frame.

"Did you spend the whole of the evening at home?" She did not answer. "Isn't it a fact that about half-past eight you went out, carrying a small parcel?"

Again she made no reply. "One of my men accidentally saw you," said Derrick Yale carelessly, "and then lost sight of you. Where did you spend the evening—you did not return to your flat until nearly eleven o'clock at night."

"I went for a walk," said Thalia Drummond coolly. "If you will give me a map of London, I will endeavour to retrace my footsteps."

"Suppose some of them have already been traced?"

Her eyes narrowed. "In that case," she said quietly, "I am saved the bother of telling you where I went."

"Now look here, Miss Drummond," he leant across the table. "I am perfectly sure that you are not, in your heart of hearts, a murderess. That word makes you wince, and it is an ugly one. But there are suspicious circumstances which I have not yet revealed to Parr about your movements last night."

"Being under suspicion is a normal condition with me," she said, "and since you know so much, it is quite unnecessary for me to tell you more."

He looked at her, but she returned his gaze without faltering, and then with a shrug of his shoulders, he said: "Really, I don't think it matters where you were."

"I'm almost inclined to agree with you," she mocked him, and went back to her office and her typewriter. "An amazing personality," thought Derrick Yale. Women did not ordinarily interest him, but Thalia Drummond was beyond and outside of the general run. Her beauty had no appeal for him; he knew she was pretty, just as he knew his office door was painted brown and that the colour of a penny stamp was red.

He took up the paper again and re-read some of the comments upon the inefficiency of police head-quarters, and soon after, as he had expected, Parr came into the room with a certain briskness and dropped into a chair.

"The Commissioner, has asked for my resignation," he said, and to the other's surprise, his voice was almost cheerful. "I'm not worrying. I intended to retire three years ago when my brother left me his money."

This was the first intimation Derrick Yale had received that Inspector Parr was a comparatively rich man.

"What are you going to do?" he asked, and Parr smiled. "In Government offices'when you are asked to resign, you resign," he said drily. "But my resignation will not take effect until the end of next month. I must wait and see what happens to you, my friend."

"To me?" said Derrick in surprise. "Oh, you mean the warning that I am to be polished off on the fourth? Let me see, there are only two or three days of life left for me," he laughed ironically as he glanced at the calendar. "I don't think you need wait for that. But, joking apart, why resign at all? Do you think if I saw the Commissioner—"

"He'd take much less notice of you than he would of a row of beans if they started articulating," said Mr. Parr. "As a matter of fact, he isn't taking me off the case until my resignation comes into effect, and I have you to thank for that."

"Me?"

The stout inspector was laughing silently.

"I told him that your life was so precious to the country that it was necessary I should remain on duty until I had got you over the fatal date," he said.

Thalia Drummond came in at that moment with another batch of correspondence.

"Good morning. Miss Drummond."

The inspector raised his eyes to the girl.

"I've been reading about you this morning," said Thalia coolly. "You're becoming quite a public character, Mr. Parr."

"Anything for the sake of a little advertisement," murmured the inspector without resentment. "It is a long time since I saw your name in the paper, Miss Drummond."

His reference to her appearance in a police court seemed to afford Thalia a great deal of amusement. "I shall have my share in time," she said. "What is the latest news about the Crimson Circle?"

"The latest news," said Mr. Parr slowly, "is that all correspondence addressed to the Crimson Circle of Mildred Street must in future be sent elsewhere."

He saw her face change; it was only a momentary flash, but the effect was very gratifying to Inspector Parr.

"Are they opening offices in the city?" she asked, recovering herself rapidly. "I don't see why they shouldn't. They seem to do almost as much as they like, and I don't see why they should not live in a very handsome block with elevators and electric signs—no, I don't think they'd better have electric signs, because even the police would see them!"

"Sarcasm in a young woman," said Mr. Parr severely, "is not only unbecoming, it is indecent!"

Yale was listening to this exchange with a delighted smile. If the girl surprised him, there were moments when Inspector Parr surprised him as much. This heavy man had a very light malicious touch when he wished.

"And where were you last night. Miss Drummond?" asked Parr, his eyes on the ground.

"In bed and dreaming," said Thalia Drummond.

"Then you must have been walking in your sleep when you were loafing about at the back of Froyant's house about half-past nine," suggested the inspector.

"So that is it, eh?" said Thalia. "You found my dainty footsteps in the garden? Mr. Yale has hinted as much already. No, inspector, I went for a walk in the park at night. The solitude is very inspiring."

Still Parr regarded the carpet attentively.

"Well, when you walk in the park, young lady, keep at some distance from Jack Beardmore, because the last time you trailed him, you scared him!"

He had hit truly this time. Her face flushed crimson and her delicate eyebrows met in a frown.

"Mr. Beardmore isn't easily scared," she said, "and besides—besides—"

Suddenly she turned and went from the room, and when Parr, after a little further conversation, also went into the outer office, she looked up at him and scowled.

"There are times, inspector, when I positively hate you!" she said vehemently.

"You surprise me," said Inspector Parr.

CHAPTER XXXII

A TRIP TO THE COUNTRY

POLICE head-quarters was on its trial. The uncomfortable amount of space which the newspapers were giving to the latest of these tragedies which were associated with the name of Crimson Circle, the questions which were on the paper to be asked in Parliament no less than the conferences behind closed doors at head-quarters, and the aloofness of all who were ordinarily connected with Inspector Parr in his work, were ominous signs which he did not fail to appreciate.

There was hardly a newspaper which did not publish a very complete list of the outrages for which the Crimson Circle was responsible, and not one which did not mention pointedly the damning fact that from the very beginning of the Circle's activity, Inspector Parr had had charge of the various cases.

He asked for, and was granted, leave to make enquiries in France. During his few days' absence, his superiors arranged for his successor. He had only one friend at head-quarters, and that curiously and strangely enough was Colonel Morton, the Commissioner in control of Parr's department.

Morton fought his case, but knew that it was a hopeless one from the beginning. In this he had the assistance of Derrick Yale. Yale made an early call at head-quarters and gave the fullest particulars with the object of exonerating his official colleague.

"The mere fact that I was on the spot, and that I had been specially engaged to protect Froyant, must take a lot of responsibility from Parr's shoulders," he urged.

The Commissioner leant back in his chair and folded his arms. "I don't want to hurt your feelings, Mr. Yale," he said bluntly, "but officially you have no existence, and I am afraid that nothing you will say is going to help Mr. Parr. He has had his chance—in fact, he has had several chances, and he has missed them."

Just as Yale was going the Commissioner beckoned him to remain.

"You can throw light upon one subject, Mr. Yale," he said. "It has reference to the killing of the man who shot James Beardmore: you remember Sibly, the sailor."

Yale nodded, and resumed the seat he had vacated.

"Who was in the cell when you were taking this man's evidence?"

"Myself, Mr. Parr and an official shorthand writer."

"Man or woman?" asked the Commissioner.

"A man. I think he was a member of your staff. And that was all. The jailer came in once or twice; in fact he came in while we were there, and brought the water, which was found afterwards to contain the poison."

The Commissioner opened a folder and selected from many documents a sheet of foolscap.

"Here is the jailer's statement," he said. "I'll save you the preliminaries, but this is what he says," said the Commissioner; he fixed his glasses and read slowly:

"The prisoner sat on his bed. Mr. Parr was sitting facing him and Mr. Yale was standing with his back to the cell door, which was open when I went in. I took a tin mug half full of water which I drew from a faucet which had been fixed for the purpose of supplying drinking water. I remember putting the tin down whilst I attended a bell call from another cell. So far as I know it was impossible that this tin could be tampered with, though it is true that the door into the yard was open. When I went into the cell Mr. Parr took the tin from my hand, and set it on a ledge near the door and told me not to interrupt them."

"You notice that no reference is made to the shorthand-writer. Was he obtained locally, do you think?"

"I'm almost sure he was from your office."

"I must ask Parr about that," said the Commissioner.

Mr. Parr (who had returned from France) when questioned on the telephone, admitted that the shorthand-writer was a local man whom he had secured by making enquiries in the little town. In the confusion which had followed the discovery that Sibly was dead, he had not thought to enquire about the man's identity.

A typewritten transcript of Sibly's statement had been given to him, and he remembered indistinctly paying the writer for his trouble. That was as far as he could help the Commissioner, whose information on the subject was not greatly increased.

Derrick Yale waited whilst this telephonic communication was in progress, and when the colonel had finished, he gathered from his dissatisfied expression that Parr's information was of no particular value.

"You don't remember the man yourself?"

Yale shook his head.

"His back was to me, most of the time," he said, "and he sat by the side of Parr."

The Commissioner muttered something about gross carelessness, and then:

"I shouldn't be surprised if your shorthand-writer was an emissary of the Crimson Circle," he said. "It was a piece of criminal neglect to have taken a man whose identity cannot be established for such an important piece of work. Yes, Parr has failed." He sighed. "I am sorry, in many ways. I like Parr. Of course, he's one of the old-fashioned police officers whom you bright outside men affect to despise, and he hasn't any extraordinary gifts, although he has been, in his time, a remarkably good officer. But he'll have to go. That is decided. I may tell you this, because I have already made the same intimation to Parr himself. It is a thousand pities."

It was no news to Vale: nor was it news to the youngest officer at police head-quarters.

But the person who seemed least concerned was Inspector Parr himself. He went about his routine work as though unconscious that any extraordinary change in his position was contemplated, and even when he met his successor, who came to look at the office he was shortly to occupy, was geniality itself.

One afternoon he met Jack Beardmore by accident in the park, and Jack was struck by the stout little man's good spirits.

"Well, inspector," said Jack, "are we any nearer the end?"

Parr nodded. "I think we are," he said. "The end of me."

This was the first definite news Jack had received of the inspector's retirement.

"But surely you're not going? You have all the threads in your hands, Mr. Parr. They can't be so foolish as to dispense with you at this very critical moment unless they have given up all hope of capturing the scoundrel."

Mr. Parr thought "they" had given up all hope long ago, but the attitude of head-quarters was a subject which he did not care to pursue.

Jack was going down to his country house. He had not visited the place since his father's death, and he would not have gone now but the necessity had arisen for revising a number of farm leases, and since the business could not be done in town, and there were other matters which needed local attention, he decided to spend a night in a place which had, in addition to the memory of this tragedy, memories almost as distasteful.

"Going down into the country are you?" said Mr. Parr thoughtfully. "Alone?"

"Yes," said Jack, and then as he guessed the other's thoughts, he asked eagerly, "You would not care to come down as my guest, would you, Mr. Parr? I should be delighted if you could, but I suppose this Crimson Circle investigation will keep you in town."

"I think they'll get on very well without me," said Mr. Parr grimly. "Yes, I think I should like to come down with you. I haven't been to the house since your poor father's death, and I should like to go over the grounds again." He asked for an additional two days' leave, and headquarters, which would have willingly dispensed with him for the remainder of his lifetime, agreed.

As Jack was leaving that night the inspector went home, packed a small Gladstone bag, and met him at the station.

Neither the weather nor the roads were conducive to a long motor-car journey, and on the whole the inspector agreed that travelling by train was more comfortable.

He had left a little note addressed to Derrick Yale, telling him where he was going, and added at the foot:

'It is possible circumstances may arise which would need my presence in town. Do not hesitate to send for me if this should be the case.'

Remembering this postscript, Mr. Parr's subsequent conduct was not a little odd.

CHAPTER XXXIII

THE POSTERS

JACK did not find him a pleasant travelling companion; the inspector had brought with him a whole bundle of newspapers, in each of which he read religiously the comments upon the Crimson Circle. His host saw what he was reading, and was astonished that the man, phlegmatic as he was, could find any pleasure in the uncomplimentary references to himself which filled the journals. He said as much. The inspector put down a paper on his knees, and took off his steel-rimmed pince-nez.

"I don't know," he said. "Criticism never did anybody any harm; it is only when a man knows he is wrong that this kind of stuff irritates him. As I happen to know I am right, it doesn't matter to me what they say."

"You really think you are right? In what respect?" asked Jack curiously, but here Parr was not offering any information. They arrived at the little station and drove the three miles which separated the line from the big gaunt house which had been James Beardmore's delight.

Jack's butler, who had come down to superintend arrangements for his master's comfort, handed a telegram to Inspector Parr almost as soon as he put his foot across the threshold. Parr looked at the face of the envelope and then at the back.

"How long has this been here?"

"It arrived about five minutes ago; a cyclist messenger brought it up from the village," he said.

The inspector tore open the envelope and extracted the form. It was signed "Derrick Yale," and read: 'Come back to London at once; most important development.'

Without a word he handed the message to the young man. "Of course you'll go. It's rather a nuisance; there isn't a train until nine o'clock," said Jack, who was disappointed at the prospect of losing his companion.

"I'm not going," said Parr calmly. "Nothing in the wide world would make me take another train journey to-night. It must wait."

This attitude toward the summons did not somehow go with Jack's perception of the inspector's character. He was, if the truth be told, secretly disappointed, although he was glad enough that Parr would share his first night in the house, every corner, every room of which, seemed to have its own especial ghost.

Parr looked at the telegram again. "He must have sent this within half-an-hour of our leaving the station," he said. "You have a telephone, haven't you?"

Jack nodded, and Parr put through a long distance call. It was a quarter of an hour before the tinkle of the bell announced that he had been connected.

Jack heard his voice in the hall, and presently the detective came in.

"As I thought," he said, "the wire was a fake. I've just been on to friend Yale."

"And did you guess it was a fake?"

Mr. Parr nodded. "I'm getting almost as good a guesser as Yale," said the detective good-humouredly. He spent the evening initiating the young man into the mysteries of picquet, of which Parr was a past-master. There is probably no more fascinating card game for two in the world than this, and so pleasantly was the evening passed, that it was with a shock that Jack looked at the clock and found it was midnight.

The room to which the inspector was shown was that which had been occupied by James Beardmore in his lifetime. It was a roomy apartment, lofty and expansive. There were three long windows, and at night the room, as the rest of the house, was lighted by means of an acetylene-gas plant which James Beardmore had installed.

"Where are you sleeping, by the way?" he said as he paused at the entrance of his room, after saying goodnight.

"I'm in the next room," said Jack, and Parr nodded and closed the door, locking it behind him.

He heard Jack's door shut, and proceeded to divest himself of part of his clothing. He made no attempt to undress, but taking from his battered suit-case an old silk dressing-gown, he wrapped it about him, turned out the light and, walking to the windows, pulled up the three blinds.

The night was fairly light; there was sufficient to enable him to find his way back to the bed, on which he lay, pulling the eiderdown over him. There is a method by which the worst cases of insomnia-haunted patients may obtain sleep, though it is one which I believe is very little known. It is to attempt deliberately to keep one's eyes open in the dark.

Mr. Parr succeeded only by turning on his side and staring out of the nearest window, which he had opened a little.

Towards morning he rose suddenly and stepped noiselessly towards the nearest window; he had heard a faint whirr of sound, a noise which a smoothly-running motorcar makes, but now there was a profound silence. He went to the washstand, and rubbed his face with cold water, drying it leisurely. Then he walked back to the window, pulled up a chair and sat so that he commanded whatever view there was of the avenue leading to the front of the house.

He had to wait nearly half an hour before he saw a dark figure steal from the shadow of the trees, only to disappear again in a deeper shadow. He momentarily glimpsed it again as it passed out of his range of vision into the shadow of the house itself. The inspector moved softly from the room and, crossing the landing, went down the stairs. The main door of the house was bolted and locked, and it was some time before he could open it. When he stepped out into the night there was nobody in sight. He crept stealthily along the path which ran parallel with the house, but found no intruder, and he had reached the main entrance again when he heard the sound of the motor fading gradually—the midnight visitor had gone.

He closed and bolted the door and went back to his room. This visit puzzled him. It was clear that the man, whoever he was, had not seen Parr, nor could he have been certain that he was under observation. He must have come and gone almost immediately.

It was not until he came down to breakfast in the morning that the mystery of the visitation was revealed. Jack was standing before the fire reading a crumpled paper which looked as if it had been posted up and torn. It was the size of a small poster and hand-printed. Before he saw its contents, Parr knew that it was a message from the Crimson Circle.

"What do you think of this?" asked Jack, looking round as the detective came in. "We found half a dozen of these posters pasted or tacked on to the trees of the drive, and this one was stuck up under my window!"

The detective read:

'Your father's debt is still unpaid. It will remain unpaid if you persuade your friends Derrick Yale and Parr to cease their activity.'

Underneath was written in smaller characters, and evidently added as an afterthought:

'We shall make no further demands upon private individuals.'

"So he was bill-posting," said Parr thoughtfully. "I wondered why he came and left so early."

"Did you see him?" asked Jack in surprise.

"I just glimpsed him. In fact, I knew he would call, though I expected a more startling consequence," said the detective.

He sat through breakfast without saying a word, except to answer the questions that Jack put to him, and then only in the briefest fashion, and it was not until they were walking across the meadows that Parr asked: "I wonder if he knows you're fond of Thalia Drummond?"

Jack went red. "Why do you ask that?" he said a little anxiously. "You don't think they will take their vengeance on Thalia, do you?"

"If it would serve his purpose, he would wipe out Thalia Drummond like that." The detective snapped his fingers. He put an end to further conversation by stopping and turning about in his tracks. "This will do," he said.

"I thought you wanted to go to the station gate—the way Marl came to the house that morning?"

Parr shook his head. "No, I wished to be sure how he approached the house. Can you point out the spot where he suddenly became so agitated?"

"Why, of course," said Jack readily, but wondering what it was all about. "It was much nearer the house; in fact, I can give you the exact spot, because I particularly remember his stepping aside from the path and ruining a young rose tree on which he put his foot. There is the tree—or one the gardener has put in its place."

He pointed, and Parr nodded his large head several times.

"This is very important," he said. He walked to where the ruined tree had been. "I knew he was lying," he said half to himself. "You cannot see the terrace from here at all. Marl told me that he saw your father standing on the terrace at the very moment he had his seizure, and my first impression was that it was the sight of your father which was responsible for his scare."

He gave Jack details of the conversation he had had with Felix Marl before his death.

"I could have corrected that," said Jack. "My father was in the library all the morning, and he did not come out of the house until we were ascending the steps of the terrace."

Parr, note-book in hand, was making a rough sketch. On his left front was the solid block of Sedgwood House, immediately before him were the gardens, enclosed by light iron railings to prevent the cattle straying on to the flower beds, and broken by the gate through which Marl must have passed. On the right was a patch of bushes, in the midst of which showed the gay top of a garden umbrella.

"Dad was very fond of the shrubbery," explained Jack. "We get high winds here even on the warmest days, and the shrubbery affords shelter. Dad used to sit there for hours reading."

Parr was slowly turning on his heel, taking in every detail of the view. Presently he nodded. "I think. I have seen all there is to be seen," he said.

As they were walking back to the house he reverted to the midnight bill-poster, and to Jack's surprise: "That was the only false move that the Crimson Circle have made, and I think it was very much an afterthought. That was not their original intention, I'll swear."

He sat down on the steps of the terrace and stared out over the landscape. Jack could not but think that a more uninspiring figure than Mr. Parr he had never met. His lack of inches, his rotundity, his large placid face, did not somehow fit in with Jack's conception of a shrewd criminal investigator. "I've got it," said Parr at last. "My first idea was right. He was coming down to blackmail you for the money your father did not pay. On his way he conceived this new idea, which is hinted at in the postscript of his message. He has decided upon some big coup, so that the reference to myself and Yale may be genuine; and he really does want us out of the game, though he'd be a fool if he did not know that the likelihood of his wishes being fulfilled in that respect are pretty remote. Let me see the poster again."

Jack brought it and the inspector spread it upon the pavement of the terrace.

"Yes, this has been written in a hurry; probably written in his car, and it is a substitute for the poster he originally intended." He rubbed his chin impatiently. "Now, what is the new scheme?" He was to learn almost immediately, for the butler came hurrying out to say that the telephone bell had been ringing in Jack's study for five minutes.

"It is you they want," said Jack, handing the receiver to the detective.

Mr. Parr took the instrument in his hands, and recognised immediately Colonel Morton's voice. "Come back to London at once, Parr; you are to attend a meeting of the Cabinet this afternoon."

Mr. Parr put down the receiver, and a smile spread over his big face.

"What is it?" asked Jack.

"I'm joining the Cabinet," said Mr. Parr, and laughed as Jack had never seen him laugh before.

CHAPTER XXXIV

BLACKMAILING A GOVERNMENT

WHEN they reached London the evening newspapers were filled with the new sensation. The Crimson Circle had indeed decided upon an ambitious programme. Briefly the story, as related in an official communique to the Press, was as follows:

That morning every member of the Government had received a typewritten document, bearing no address and no other indication of its origin save a Crimson Circle stamped on every page. The document ran:

'Every effort of your police, both official and private, the genius of Mr. Derrick Yale, and the plodding efforts of Chief Inspector Parr have failed to check Our activity. The full story of Our success is not known. It has been unfortunately Our unpleasant duty to remove a number of people from life, not so much in a spirit of vengeance, as to serve as a salutary warning to others, and only this morning it has been Our unhappy duty to remove Mr. Samuel Heggitt, a lawyer, who was engaged by the late Harvey Froyant on particular work, in the course of which he came unpleasantly close to Our identity. Fortunately for the other members of his firm, he undertook that task personally. His body will be found by the side of the railway between Buxton and Marsden.'

Since the police are unable to hold Us, and since We are in complete agreement with those in authority who say that We are the most dangerous menace to society that exists, We have agreed to forego Our activities on condition that the sum of a million pounds sterling is placed at Our disposal. The method by which this money shall be transferred will be detailed later. This must be accompanied by a free pardon in blank, so that We may, if occasion necessitates, or hereinafter Our identity is disclosed, avail Ourselves of that document.'

Refusal to agree to Our terms will have unpleasant consequences. We name hereunder twelve eminent Parliamentarians, who must stand as hostages for the fulfilment of Our desire. If, at the end of the week, the Government have not agreed to Our terms, one of these gentlemen will be removed.'

The first person that Parr met on his arrival at Whitehall was Derrick Yale, and for once the famous detective looked worried.

"I was afraid of this development," he said, "and the queer thing is that it has come at a moment when I thought I was in a position to lay my hand on the chief offender."

He took Parr's hand in his, and walked him along the gloomy corridor.

"This spoils my day's fishing," he said, and Inspector Parr remembered.

"Of course, to-day is the day you die! But I suppose you are reprieved under the general amnesty which the Crimson Circle have issued," he said drily, and his companion laughed.

"I want to tell you, before we go into this meeting, that I am willing to place myself unreservedly at your disposal," he said quietly. "I think you ought to know, Parr, that the present wishes of the Cabinet are to give me an official status and place the whole of the investigations in my charge. I have been sounded on the matter, and have given them point-blank refusal. I am convinced that you are the best man for the job, and I will serve under no other chief."

"Thank you," said Parr simply. "Perhaps the Cabinet will take another view."

The Cabinet meeting was held in the Secretary of State's office; all the recipients of the Crimson Circle's memo were present from the beginning, but it was some time before outsiders were called in. Yale was summoned first, and a quarter of an hour later the messenger beckoned the inspector.

Inspector Parr knew most of the illustrious gathering by sight, and being on the opposite side in politics, had no particular respect for any. He felt an air of hostility as he came into the big room, and the chilly nod which the white-bearded Prime Minister gave him in response to his bow, confirmed this impression.

"Mr. Parr," said the Prime Minister icily, "we are discussing the question of the Crimson Circle, which, as you must realise, has become almost a national problem. Their dangerous character has been emphasised by a memorandum which has been addressed to the various members of the Cabinet by this infamous association, and which, I have no doubt, you have read in the newspapers."

"Yes, sir," said the inspector.

"I will not disguise from you the fact that we are profoundly dissatisfied with the course which our investigations have taken. Although you have had every facility and every power granted you, including—" he consulted a paper before him, but Parr interrupted him.

"I should not like you to tell the meeting what powers I have received, Prime Minister," he said firmly, "or what particular privileges have been granted me by the Secretary of State."

The Prime Minister was taken aback.

"Very well," he said. "I will add that, although you have had extraordinary privileges, and opportunities, and you have even been present when the outrages have taken place, you have not succeeded in bringing the criminal to justice." The inspector nodded. "It was our original wish to place the matter in the hands of Mr. Derrick Yale, who has been especially successful in tracing two of the murderers, without, however, being able to bring the prime culprit to justice. Mr. Yale, however, refuses to accept the commission unless you are in control. He has kindly expressed his willingness to serve under you, and in this course we arc agreed. I understand that your resignation is already before the Commissioners, and that it has been formally accepted. That acceptance, for the time being, is reserved. Now remember, Mr. Parr," the Prime Minister leant forward and spoke very earnestly and emphatically: "It is absolutely impossible that we can accede to the Crimson Circle's demands: such a course would be the negation of all law, and the surrender of all authority. We rely upon you to afford to every member of the Government who is threatened, that protection which is his right as a citizen. Your whole career is in the balance."

The inspector, thus dismissed, rose slowly. "If the Crimson Circle keeps its word," he said, "I guarantee that not a hair of one member of your Government shall be harmed in London. Whether I can capture the man who describes himself as the Crimson Circle, remains to be seen."

"I suppose," said the Prime Minister, "there is no doubt that this unfortunate man, Heggitt, has been killed."

It was Derrick Yale who answered. "No, sir; the body was found early this morning. Mr. Heggitt, who lives at Marsden, left London last night by train, and apparently the crime was committed en route."

"It is deplorable, deplorable." The Prime Minister shook his head. "A terrible orgy of murder and crime, and it seems that we are not at the end of it yet."

When they came out into Whitehall, Yale and his companion found that a large crowd had gathered, for news had leaked out that a meeting was being held to discuss this new and extraordinary problem which confronted the Government.

Yale, who was recognised, was cheered, but Inspector Parr passed unnoticed through the crowd—to his intense relief.

Undoubtedly the Crimson Circle was the sensation of the hour. Some of the evening newspaper placards bore a crimson circle in imitation of the famous insignia of the gang, and wherever men met, there the possibility of the Circle carrying their threat into effect was discussed.

Thalia Drummond looked up as her employer came in. The evening newspaper was in front of her, and her chin rested on her clasped hands, and she read every line, word by word. Derrick noticed the interest, and observed, too, her momentary confusion as she folded the paper and put it away.

"Well, Miss Drummond, what do you think of their last exploit?"

"It is colossal," she said. "In some respects, admirable."

He looked at her gravely.

"I confess I can see little to admire," he said. "You take rather a queer, twisted view of things."

"Don't I?" she said coolly. "You must never forget, Mr. Yale, that I have a queer, twisted mind."

He paused at the door of his room and looked back at her, a long, keen scrutiny, which she met without so much as an eyelid quivering.

"I think you should be very grateful that Mr. Johnson, of Mildred Street, no longer receives your interesting communications," he said, and she was silent.

He came out again soon after. "I am probably going to establish my offices at police head-quarters," he said, "and realising that that atmosphere is one in which you will not nourish, I am leaving you here in control of my ordinary business."

"Are you accepting the responsibility for capturing the Crimson Circle?" she asked steadily.

He shook his head. "Inspector Parr is in control," he said, "but I am going to help him."

He made no further reference to his new task, and the rest of the morning was spent in routine work. He went out to lunch and said he would not be back that day, giving her instructions regarding letters he wished despatched.

He had hardly gone before his telephone bell went, and at the sound of the voice at the other end, she nearly dropped the receiver.

"Yes, it is I," she said. "Good morning, Mr. Beardmore."

"Is Yale there?" asked Jack.

"He has just gone out: he will not be back to-day. If there is anything important to tell him, I may be able to find him," she said, steadying her voice with an effort.

"I don't know whether it's important or not," said Jack, "but I was going through my father's papers this morning, a very disagreeable job, by the way, and I found a whole bunch of papers relating to Marl."

"To Marl?" she said slowly.

"Yes, apparently poor Dad knew a great deal more about Marl than we imagined. He had been in prison: did you know that?"

"I could have guessed it," said Thalia.

"Father always put through an inquiry about people before he did business with them," Jack went on, "and apparently there is a lot of explanation about Marl's early life, collected by a French agency. He seems to have been a pretty bad lot, and I wonder the governor had dealings with him. One curious document is an envelope which is marked 'Photograph of Execution': it was sealed up by the French people, and apparently the governor didn't open it. He hated gruesome things of that kind."

"Have you opened it?" she asked quickly.

"No," he answered in a tone of surprise. "Why do you jump at me like that?"

"Will you do me a favour, Jack?" It was the first time she had ever called him by name, and she could almost see him redden.

"Why—why, of course, Thalia, I'd do anything for you." he said eagerly.

"Don't open the envelope," she said intensely. "Keep all the papers relating to Marl in a safe place. Will you promise that?"

"I promise," he said. "What a queer request to make!"

"Have you told anybody about it?" she asked.

"I sent a note to Inspector Parr."

He heard her exclamation of annoyance. "Will you promise me not to tell anybody, especially about the photograph?"

"Of course, Thalia," he answered. "I'll send it along to you, if you like."

"No, no, don't do that," she said, then abruptly she finished the conversation.

She sat for a few minutes breathing quickly, and then she rose, and putting on her hat, she locked up the office, and went to lunch.

CHAPTER XXXV

THALIA LUNCHES WITH A CABINET MINISTER

THE fourth of the month had passed, and Derrick Yale was still alive. He commented on the fact as he came into the office which he and Inspector Parr jointly occupied. "Incidentally," he said, "I have lost my fishing."

Parr grunted. "It is better that you lost your fishing than that we lost sight of you," he said. "I am perfectly convinced that if you had taken that trip, you would never have returned."

Yale laughed. "You have a tremendous faith in the Crimson Circle, and their ability to keep their promises."

"I have—to a point," said the inspector, without looking up from the letter he was writing.

"I hear that Brabazon has made a statement to the police," said Yale, after an interval.

"Yes," said the inspector. "Not a very informative one, but a statement of sorts. He has admitted that for a long time he was changing the money which the Crimson Circle extracted from their victims, though he was unaware of the fact. He also gives particulars of his joining the Circle, after which, of course, he acted as a conscious agent."

"Are you charging him with the murder of Marl?"

Inspector Parr shook his head. "We haven't sufficient evidence for that," he said, blotted his letter, folded it and enclosed it in an envelope.

"What did you discover in France? I have not had an opportunity of talking to you about that," asked Yale.

Parr leant back in his chair, felt for his pipe, and lit it before he answered.

"About as much as poor old Froyant discovered," he said. "In fact, I followed very closely the same line of investigation that he had. It was mostly and mainly about Marl and his iniquities. You know that he was a member of a criminal gang in France, and that he and his companion, Lightman—I think that was the name—were condemned to death. Lightman should have died, but the executioners bungled the job, and he was sent off to Devil's Island, or Cayenne, or one of those French settlements, where he died."

"He escaped," said Yale quietly.

"The devil he did." Mr. Parr looked up. "Personally, I wasn't so interested in Lightman as I was in Marl."

"Do you speak French, Parr?" asked Yale suddenly.

"Fluently," was the reply, and the inspector looked up. "Why do you ask?"

"I have no reason, except that I wondered how you pursued your inquiries."

"I speak French—very well," said Parr, and would have changed the subject.

"And Lightman escaped," said Yale softly. "I wonder where he is now."

"That is a question I have never troubled to ask myself." There was a note of impatience in the inspector's voice.

"You were not the only person interested in Marl, apparently. I saw a note on your desk from young Beardmore, saying that he had discovered some papers relating to the late Felix. His father had also made inquiries about the man. Of course, James Beardmore would. He was a cautious man."

He was lunching with the Commissioner, Mr. Parr learnt, and was not at all hurt that he was excluded from the invitation. He was very busy in these days, selecting the men who were to form the bodyguard o the Cabinet, and he could well afford to miss engagements which invariably bored him.

As it happens, his company would have been a great embarrassment, for Yale had something to communicate to the Commissioner, something which it was not well that Inspector Parr should hear. It was near to the end of the meal that he dropped his bombshell, and it was so effective that the Commissioner fell back in his chair and gasped.

"Somebody at police head-quarters," he said incredulously. "Why, that is impossible, Mr. Yale."

Derrick Yale shook his head. "I wouldn't say anything was impossible, sir," he said, "but doesn't it seem to you that all the evidence tends to support that idea? Every effort that we make to bring about the undoing of the Crimson Circle is anticipated. Somebody having access to the cell of Sibly, killed him. Who but a person having authority from head-quarters? Take the case of Froyant: there were a number of detectives on duty round and about the house; nobody apparently came in and nobody went out."

The Commissioner was calmer now. "Let us have this thing clear, Mr. Yale," he said. "Are you accusing Parr?"

Derrick Yale laughed and shook his head. "Why, of course not," he said. "I cannot imagine Parr having a single criminal instinct. Only if you will think the matter out," he leant over the table and lowered his voice, "and will go into every detail and every crime that the Crimson Circle has committed, you cannot fail to be struck by this fact: that, hovering in the background all the time was somebody in authority."

"Parr?" said the Commissioner.

Derrick Yale bit his lower lip thoughtfully. "I don't want to think of Parr," he said. "I would rather think of him as being victimised by a subordinate he trusts. You quite understand," he went on quickly, "that I should not hesitate to accuse Parr if my discoveries took me in that direction. I would not even free you, sir, from suspicion, if you gave me cause."

The Commissioner looked uncomfortable. "I can assure you that I know nothing whatever about the Crimson Circle," he said gruffly, and realising the absurdity of his protest, laughed.

"Who is that girl over there?" he pointed to a couple who were dining in a corner of the big restaurant. "She keeps looking across toward you."

"That girl," said Mr. Derrick Yale carefully, "is a young lady named Thalia Drummond, and her companion, unless I am greatly mistaken, is the Honourable Raphael Willings, a member of the Government and one who has been threatened by the Crimson Circle."

"Thalia Drummond?" The Commissioner whistled. "Isn't she the young person who was in very serious trouble some time ago? She was Froyant's secretary, was she not?"

The other nodded.

"She is an enigma to me," he said, shaking his head, "and the greatest mystery of all is her nerve. At this precise moment she is supposed to be sitting in my office answering telephone calls and dealing with any correspondence which may arrive."

"You employ her, do you?" asked the astonished Commissioner, and then with a little smile, "I agree with you about her nerve, but how does a girl of that class come to be acquainted with Mr. Willings?"

Here Derrick Yale was not prepared to supply an answer.

He was still sitting with the Commissioner when he saw the girl rise and, followed by her companion, walk slowly down the room. Her way led her past his table, and she met his enquiring glance with a smile and a little nod, and said something over her shoulder to the middle-aged man who was following her.

"How is that for nerve?" asked Derrick.

"I should imagine you'd have something to say to the young lady," was the Commissioner's only comment. Derrick Yale was very seldom conventional, either in his speech or his behaviour, but for once he found it difficult to deal with a painful situation other than in the time-honoured way.

The girl had reached the office a few minutes before him, and she was taking off her hat when he came in.

"One moment, Miss Drummond," he said. "I have a few words to say to you before you continue your work. Why were you away from the office at lunch time? I particularly asked you to be here,"

"And Mr. Willings particularly asked me to go to lunch," said Thalia with an innocent smile, "and as he is a member of the Government, I am sure you would not have liked me to refuse."

"How did you come to know Mr. 'Willings?"

She looked at him up and down with that cool, insolent glance of hers.

"There are many ways one may meet men," she said. "One may advertise for them in the matrimonial newspapers, or one may meet them in the park, or one may be introduced to them. I was introduced to Mr. Willings."

"When?"

"This morning," she said, "at about two o'clock. I sometimes go to dances at Merros Club," she explained. "It is the relaxation which my youth excuses. That is where we became acquainted."

Yale took some money from his pocket and laid it on the desk.

"There is your week's wages. Miss Drummond," he said without heat. "I shall not require your services after this afternoon."

She raised her eyebrows. "Aren't you going to reform me?" she asked him so seriously that he was taken aback. Then he laughed.

"You're beyond reformation. There are many things I will excuse, and had there been a serious shortage in the petty cash, I could have overlooked that. But I cannot allow you to leave my office when I give you explicit instructions to stay here."

She picked up the money and counted it. "Exactly the sum," she mocked. "You must be Scottish, Mr. Yale."

"There is only one way that you could be reformed, Thalia Drummond." His voice was very earnest, and he seemed to experience a difficulty in finding the right words.

"And what is that, pray?"

"For a man to marry you. I'm almost inclined to make the experiment."

She sat on the edge of the desk and rocked with silent laughter.

"You are funny," she said at last, "and now I see that you are a true reformer." She was solemnity itself now. "Confess, Mr. Yale, that you only look upon me as an experiment, and that you have no more affection for me than I have for that aged and decrepit blue-bottle crawling up the wall."

"I'm not in love with you, if that is what you mean."

"I did mean something of the sort," she said. "No, on the whole, I think I'll take my dismissal and my week's wages, and thank you for giving me the opportunity of meeting and serving such a brilliant genius."

He ended the conversation as though he had made some business proposal which had been declined, and said something about giving her a reference, and there the matterended for him. He went into his office, and did not even do her the honour of slamming the door after him.

And yet her dismissal was a serious matter for Thalia. It meant one of two things. Either that Derrick Yale seriously suspected her—and that was the gravest possibility to her—or else that her discharge was only a ruse, part of a deeper plan to bring about her undoing.

On her way home she recalled his reference to Johnson of Mildred Street. There might be something behind that beyond the revelation of the fact that he knew she was associated with the Crimson Circle, and he wanted her to know he knew.

When she reached her flat there was a letter waiting for her, as there had been on the previous night. The controlling spirit of the Crimson Circle was an assiduous correspondent as far as she was concerned. In the privacy of her own room she tore open the envelope.

'You did well,' (the letter ran). 'You have carried out my instructions to the letter. The introduction to Willings was well managed and, as I promised you, there was no difficulty. I wish you to know this man thoroughly and discover what are his little weaknesses. Particularly do I wish to know his attitude of mind and the real attitude of the Cabinet towards my proposal. The dress you wore at lunch to-day was not quite good enough. Do not spare expense in the matter of costume. Derrick Yale is dismissing you this afternoon, but that need not trouble you, for there is no further need for you to stay in his office. You are dining to-night with Willings. He is particularly susceptible to feminine charms. If possible, let him invite you to his house. He has a collection of ancient swords of which he is very proud. You will then be able to discover the lay of the house.'

She looked into the envelope. There were two crisp notes for a hundred pounds, and as she put them into her little hand-bag her face was very grave.

CHAPTER XXXVI

THE CIRCLE MEETS

MR. RAPHAEL WILLINGS was a product of his age. Though he was still in the early forties, he had pushed himself into Cabinet rank by the sheer force of his character. To describe him as a popular Minister would be to stretch the truth beyond permissible bounds. He was neither popular with his colleagues, nor with the country who, whilst recognising his remarkable powers and acclaiming him as the greatest of the parliamentary orators, nevertheless distrusted him. He had given so many proofs of his insincerity that it was remarkable that he should have attained to the position he occupied.

But he had a number of followers. Men who were unwavering in their faith, who could be depended upon to vote steadily at the lift of his finger, and the Government majority was too small to risk the exclusion of the Willings' bloc.

Amongst his colleagues he had a bad name. It is not necessary to particularise the circumstances which produced his reputation, but it is a notorious fact that he escaped appearing in an unsavoury divorce case by the skin of his teeth. So unpopular was he that twice Merros Club and a fashionable night club of which he was a member and an habitue, were raided by the police in the hope of compromising this nighty politician. The raid had been planned by the wife of one of his colleagues, and that Willings was not unaware of the fact, was proved when the newspaper he owned aimed a bitter attack on the lady's unfortunate husband, an attack so worded, so framed, that the Minister retired from public life.

A well-built man inclined to plumpness, slightly bald, there was no gainsaying his personal charm. He was under the impression that his introduction to Thalia Drummond had been skillfully manoeuvred by himself. He would have been horrified to know that the lady who introduced him had received instructions that morning from the Crimson Circle to bring the introduction about. The Crimson Circle had its agents in all branches of life and in all classes. There were book-keepers, there was at least one railway director, there was a doctor and three chefs d'hotel amongst the hundred who obeyed the call of the Crimson Circle. They were well paid and their duties were not onerous. Sometimes, as in this case, they had no more to do than to bring about an introduction between two people whom the Crimson Circle desired to meet, but in every case their instructions came to them in exactly in every the same form.

The organisation of this great force was extraordinarily complete. In some uncanny way the chief of the Crimson Circle had smelt penury and disaster almost as soon as the recipients of these two evil factors were aware that they were present. One by one they had been absorbed, each ignorant of the other's identity, and profoundly ignorant of their master. He had come to them in strange places and circumstances. Each had his own function to perform, and generally the part which was played by the subordinate members of the league was ludicrously simple and unimportant.

A few members of the Circle had, in a panic, made statements to police head-quarters, and from them it was learned how simple were some of the tasks which were given out by the mystery man.

From fear of the tragic consequences of disloyalty, the majority of the Crimson Circle remained loyal to their unknown chief, and it was a remarkable tribute to his system of espionage, that when he sent forth his summons, as he did on the day Derrick Yale lunched with the Commissioner, calling every member of the Crimson Circle to the first meeting they had ever held, giving them the most explicit instructions as to the garb they should wear, and the means they should adopt to avoid disclosing themselves to their fellows, he omitted the waverers and the malcontents as though their very thoughts were written plainly before him. To Thalia Drummond that meeting will always remain the most vivid and poignant memory of her association with the Crimson Circle.

The city contains many old churches, but none anterior in date to the church of St. Agnes on Powder Hill. It had escaped the ravages of the Great Fire, only to be smothered under by the busy city which had grown up about it. Enclosed by tall warehouses, so that its squat steeple was absent from the sky-line, it had a congregation which might be numbered on the fingers of two hands, although it supported a vicar who preached punctiliously every week to a congregation which was practically paid to attend. Once a churchyard had surrounded it, and the bones of the faithful had been laid to peace within its shadow, but the avaricious city, grudging so much waste building land, had passed Acts which had removed the bones to a more salubrious situation and had covered the place of family vaults with office buildings.

Entrance to the church was up an alley which led from a side passage and the figures which slunk along the unlighted way seemed to melt through the almost invisible doors into a gloom even thicker than the night.

For in the church of St. Agnes the Crimson Circle held the first and last meeting of his servitors.

Here, again, his organisation was marvellous. Every member of his company had received explicit orders telling him to the very minute when he must arrive, so that no two came together. How he obtained the keys of the church; what careful manoeuvring he must have planned to bring the hour of meeting and the dispersal between the two periods when the lane would be patrolled by the City police, Thalia Drummond could only guess.

She came into the alley-way punctually, went up the two steps to a door which opened as she approached and was closed immediately she entered the lobby. There was no light of any kind, save for the faint light of night which filtered through a stained-glass window.

"Go straight ahead," whispered a voice. "You will take the end of the second pew on the right."

There were other people in the church. She could just distinguish them, two in each pew, a silent, ghostly congregation, none speaking to the other. Presently the man who had admitted her came into the church and walked to the altar rails, and at the first words she knew that the servants of the Crimson Circle sat in the presence of their master.

His voice was low and muffled and hollow; she guessed he wore the veil she had seen over his head the first night she had met him.

"My friends," he said, and she heard every word, "the time has come when our society will be dispersed. You have read my offer in the public press; and you are interested to this extent, that I intend distributing at least twenty per cent. of the money which the

Government must eventually give me amongst those who have served me. If there are any here who are nervous that we shall be interrupted, let me assure them that the police patrol does not pass for another quarter of an hour, and that it is quite impossible for the sound of my voice to reach outside the church."

He raised his voice a little, and there was a hard note in it when he added:

"And to those who may have treachery in their hearts, and imagine that so widely announced a meeting might bring about my undoing, let me say that it is impossible that I shall be captured to-night. Ladies and gentlemen, I will not disguise from you that we are in considerable danger. Facts which may enable the police to identify me have on two occasions come to light. I have upon my tracks Derrick Yale, who I will not deny is a source of considerable anxiety to me, and Inspector Parr"—he paused—"who is not to be despised. In this supreme moment I do not hesitate to call upon every one of you for an extraordinary effort of assistance. To-morrow you will each receive operation orders prepared in such detail that it will be impossible for you to misunderstand any particular requirement I have made known. Remember that you are as much in danger as I," he said more softly, "and your reward shall be correspondingly great. Now you will pass out of the church one by one, at thirty seconds interval, beginning with the first two on the right, continuing with the first two on the left. Go!"

At intervals these dark figures glided along the aisle and vanished through the door to the left of the pulpit.

The man at the chancel rails waited until the church was empty and then he, too, passed through the door into the lobby and into the passage.

He locked the outer door and slipped the key into his pocket. The church clock was booming the half-hour when he called a taxi-cab and was driven westward.

Thalia Drummond had preceded him by a quarter of an hour, and in the taxi which carried her to the same end of the town she brought about a lightning transformation of her appearance. The old black raincoat which covered her to the throat, the heavy-veiled black hat, were taken off. Beneath it she wore a cloak of delicate silk tissue, covering an evening dress which would have satisfied her apparently exigent master.

She took off her hat and tidied her hair as well as she could, and when she stepped down at the flashing entrance of Merros Club and handed a small attache case to the bowing attendant, she was a picture of radiant loveliness.

So jack Beardmore thought. He was supping with some friends much against his will, for he hated the night side of life, when he saw her come in, and scowled jealously at her debonair escort.

"Who is he?"

Jack's companion glanced across lazily.

"I don't know the lady," he said, "but the man is Raphael Willings. He is a big pot in the Government."

Thalia Drummond had seen the young man before he had seen her, and she groaned inwardly. Half of what her host said she missed; her mind was completely absorbed in other directions, and it was not until a familiar phrase reached her ear that she turned her interest toward the Minister.

"Antique swords," she said with a start. "I'm told you have a wonderful collection, Mr. Willings."

"Are you interested?" he smiled.

"A little. In fact, quite a lot," she said awkwardly, and it was not like Thalia to be at a loss for a reply.

"Could I ask you to come along to tea one day and see them?" said Raphael. "One doesn't often find a woman who is interested in such things. Shall we say to-morrow?"

"Not to-morrow," said Thalia hastily. "Perhaps the next day."

He made the appointment then and there, writing it ostentatiously on his cuff.

She saw Jack leave the club without a look in her direction, and she felt absurdly miserable. She did so want to talk to him and was praying that he would come over to their table.

Mr. Willings insisted upon driving her home in his car, and she left him with a sigh of relief. He did not harmonise with her mood that night.

There was a little forecourt to the flats in which she lived, and she had dismissed her admirer (he made no secret of this relationship) in the street outside. She had to walk a dozen paces to reach one of the two entrances, and even before she had sent her escort away, she was aware that a man was waiting for her in the darkened court.

She stood on the pavement until Willings's car had moved on, and then she came slowly toward the waiting man. He spoke for a minute in a voice that was a little above a whisper, and she responded in the same tone.

The conversation was of very short duration. Presently the man turned without sign or word of farewell, and walked quickly away and the girl entered her flat.

Though the man made no sign, he knew he was being followed. He had been waiting for ten minutes in the dark of the forecourt and had seen the stealthy figure in the doorway of a closed shop opposite the flats. Apparently, however, he was oblivious of the fact that somebody was walking behind him, somebody he knew would presently overtake him and look into his face. He turned into a side thoroughfare where the street lamps were few and far between, and as he did so he slackened his pace. Presently the spy overtook him, choosing for the point of passing, a place within the radius of a lamp. He had bent his head to peer into the first man's face when suddenly the quarry turned and sprang at him. The trailer was taken by surprise; before he could shout, a grip of iron was around his throat and he was flung half-senseless to the stone pavement. And then from nowhere in particular, appeared as by magic three men, who pounced upon the prostrate tracker and jerked him to his feet.

He glared round, dazed and shaken, and his eyes fell upon the man he had been set to watch. "My God!" he gasped. "I know you!"

The other smiled. "You will never be able to employ your information, my friend," he said.

CHAPTER XXXVII

"I WILL SEE YOU—IF YOU ARE ALIVE"

JACK BEARDMORE went home savage and sick at heart. Thalia Drummond was an obsession to him, and yet he had every reason to believe the worst of her. He was a fool, a thrice-condemned fool, he told himself as he paced the library, his hands thrust into his pockets, his handsome young face clouded with the gloom of despair. He felt at that moment he would like to hurt her, punish her as she unconsciously had punished him. He flung himself down into his chair and sat for an hour with his head on his hands, covering the old ground which reason had so often trodden that it had left a worn and familiar track.

He got up sick and weary, and, opening a safe, took out a packet of documents and flung them on the table. It was the sealed envelope addressed to his father and unopened which interested him most, and he had a childish desire to open it if only to spite Thalia.

Why was she so anxious that he should not see the photograph which it contained? Was she so interested in Marl? He remembered with a scowl that she had spent the evening with that man on the night he died so mysteriously. He rose, and gathering the papers together, he carried them to his bedroom. He was so tired that he had not even the curiosity to probe into the mystery which attached to the photograph of an execution. He shivered at the thought of the grisly contents, and he dropped the package on his dressing-table with a little grimace and began leisurely to undress. He quite expected that he would pass a sleepless night; his emotion and the state of his mind seemed to call for such an end to a miserable day, but youth, if it has its anguish, has also its natural reaction. He was asleep almost as soon as his head touched the pillow. And then he began to dream. To dream of Thalia Drummond; and in his dream, Thalia was in the power of an ogre whose face was remarkably like Inspector Parr's. He dreamt of Marl, a grotesque terrifying figure, whom he somehow associated with Inspector Parr's grandmother—that "mother" of whom he stood in such awe.

What woke him was the reflection of a light from the dressing-table mirror. The light had been extinguished when he sat up in bed, but, half-asleep as he was, he was certain that there had been a flash of some kind—it was hardly the season for lightning.

"Who is there?" he asked, and put out his hand to reach for the lamp. But the lamp was not there; somebody had moved it. Now he saw, and was out of bed in a second.

He heard a movement toward the door and ran. Somebody was in his grip, somebody who squirmed and struggled, and then he released his hold with a gasp. It was a woman—instinct told him that it was Thalia Drummond.

Slowly he put out his hand, groping for the electric switch, and the room was flooded with light.

It was Thalia—Thalia as white as death and trembling. Thalia who held something behind her and met his pained gaze with a tragic attempt at defiance. "Thalia!" he groaned, and sat down. "Thalia in his room! What had she been doing? Why did you come?" he asked shakily, "and what are you concealing?"

"Why did you bring those papers up to your room?" she asked almost fiercely. "If you had left them in your safe—oh, why didn't you leave them in your safe?" And now he saw that she held the sealed packet containing the photograph of the execution.

"But—but, Thalia," he stammered, "I don't understand you. Why didn't you tell me—"

"I told you not to look at the picture. I never dreamt you would bring it here. They have been here to-night searching for it."

She was breathless, on the verge of tears that were not all anger.

"Been here to-night?" he said slowly. "Who have been here?"

"The Crimson Circle. They knew you had that photograph, and they came and burgled your library. I was in the house when they came, and prayed—prayed "—she wrung her hands and he saw the look of anguish on her face. "I prayed that they would find it, and now they will think you have seen the picture. Oh, why did you do it?"

He reached for his dressing-gown, realising that his attire was somewhat scanty, and in the warm folds he felt a little more assurance.

"You are still talking Greek to me," he said. "The thing I understand perfectly is that my house has been burgled. Will you come with me?"

She followed him down the stairs and into his library.

She had spoken the truth. The door of the safe hung drunkenly upon its hinges. A hole had been cut through the shutter and it was open. The contents of the safe lay upon the floor; the drawers of his desk had been forced open and apparently a search had been made amongst the papers on the desk. Even the waste-paper basket had been turned out and searched.

"I can't understand it," he muttered. He was pulling the heavy curtains across the window.

"You will understand better, though I hope you do not understand too well," she said grimly. "Now, please take a sheet of paper and write as I dictate."

"To whom must I write?" he asked in surprise.

"Inspector Parr," she said. "Say 'Dear Inspector.—Here is the photograph which my father received the day before his death. I have not opened it, but perhaps it may interest you.'"

Meekly he wrote as she ordered and signed the letter, which, with the photograph, she put into a large envelope. "And now address it," she said. "And write on it on the top left-hand corner, 'From John Beardmore,' and put after that 'Photograph, very urgent.'"

With the envelope in her hand she walked to the door. "I shall see you to-morrow, Mr. Beardmore, if you are alive."

He would have laughed, but there was something in her drawn face, some message in her quivering lips, that checked the laughter on his.

CHAPTER XXXVIII

THE ARREST OF THALIA

IT was the seventh day following the meeting of the Cabinet, and, so far from agreeing with the terms of the Crimson Circle, the Government had made it known, in the most unmistakable terms, that it refused to deal with the Circle or its emissaries.

That afternoon Mr. Raphael Willings prepared for a visitor. His house in Onslow Gardens was one of the show places of the country. His collection of antique armour and swords, his priceless intaglios and his rare prints were without equal in the world. But he had no thought of his visitor's antiquarian interests when he made his preparations, and he was less deterred than stimulated by a confidential document which had come to him, intimating in plain language the character which Thalia Drummond bore.

Thief she might be—well, she could take any sword in the armoury, any print on the wall, the rarest intaglio among his show cases, so long as she was pleasant and complacent.

When Thalia came she was admitted by a foreign-looking footman and remembered that Raphael Willings had only Italian servants in the house.

Warily she surveyed the room into which she was ushered. There were open windows at each end—which surprised her. She had expected to find a little tete-a-tete tea table. That was missing, and yet in this room was the cream of his collection, as she could see at a glance. Willings came in a few seconds later, and greeted her warmly.

"Eat, drink, and be merry, for to-morrow we die; perhaps to-day," he said melodramatically. "Have you heard the news?"

She shook her head. "I am the newest victim of the Crimson Circle," he said gaily enough. "You probably read the newspapers, and know all about that famous company. Yes," he went on with a laugh, "of all my colleagues I have the honour to be the first chosen for sacrifice; pour encourager les autres."

She could not help wondering how, in these circumstances, Ralph Willings could preserve so unruffled a mien.

"As the tragedy is due to occur in this house some time this afternoon," he was continuing, "I must ask you to extend your kindness—" There was a tap at the door, and a servant came in to say something in Italian, which the girl did not understand.

Raphael nodded. "My car is at the door, if you would honour me, we will have tea at my little place in the country. We shall be there in half-an-hour."

This was a development she had not looked for. "Where is your little place in the country?" she asked.

It was, he explained, between Barnet and Hatfield, and expatiated on the loveliness of Hertfordshire.

"I prefer to have tea here," she said, but he shook his head.

"Believe me, my dear young lady," he said earnestly, "the threat of the Crimson Circle distresses me not at all, Onslow Gardens is 'paradise enow' with so delightful a guest, but the police have been to see me this afternoon, and have changed all my plans. I told them that I had a friend coming to tea, and they suggested a more public rendezvous. The police, however, quite approve of my alternative scheme. Now, Miss Drummond, you are not going to spoil a very happy afternoon? I owe you a thousand apologies, but I shall be very disappointed if you refuse: I have sent two of my servants down to have everything in readiness, and I hope to be able to show you one of the loveliest little houses within a hundred miles of London."

She nodded. "Very well," she said, and when he had gone, she strolled through the room examining its fascinating contents with every appearance of interest.

He came back wearing his greatcoat, and found her looking at a section of the wall which was covered with beautiful examples of the Eastern swordmaker's art.

"They're lovely, aren't they? I'm so sorry I can't explain the history of them," he said, and then in a changed tone: "Who has taken the Assyrian dagger?"

There was undoubtedly a blank space in the wall where a weapon had hung, and a little label beneath the empty space was sufficient to call attention to its absence.

"I was wondering the same thing," said the girl.

Mr. Willings frowned. "Perhaps one of the servants have taken it down," he suggested. "Though I have given them strict instructions that they are not to be cleaned except under my personal directions." He hesitated, and then: "I'll see about that when I come back," he said, and he ushered her out of the room into the waiting limousine.

She could see that the loss of his precious trophy had disturbed him, for some of his animation had departed.

"I can't understand it," he said as they were passing through Barnet. "I know the dagger was there yesterday, because I was showing it to Sir Thomas Summers. He is keenly interested in Eastern steel work. None of the servants would dare touch the swords."

"Perhaps you've had strangers in the room."

He shook his head. "Only the gentleman from police head-quarters," he said, "and I'm quite sure he wouldn't have taken it. No, it is a little mystery which we can put on one side at the moment."

For the rest of the journey he was attentive, polite, and mildly amusing. Not once did he give the slightest hint that he entertained any other emotion towards her than that of a well-bred man for a respected guest.

He had not exaggerated the charms of his "little place" on the Hatfield Road. In truth, it lay nearly three miles from the main road, and was delightfully situated in the midst of rolling and wooded country.

"Here we are," he said, as he led her through a panelled hall into an exquisitely decorated little drawing room. Tea was laid, but there was no servant in sight. "And now, my dear," said Willings, "we are alone, thank heaven."

His tone, his very manner had changed, and the girl knew that the critical moment was at hand. Yet her hand did not tremble as she filled the teapot from the steaming kettle, seemingly oblivious to all that he was saying. She had poured out the tea and was setting his cup in its place, when, without preliminary, he stooped over her and kissed her; another second, and she was in his arms.

She did not struggle, but her grave eyes were fixed steadfastly on his, and she said quietly: "I have something I'd like to say to you."

"Well, you can say anything you wish, my dear," said the amorous Willings, holding her tightly, and looking into her unflinching eyes.

Before she could speak again his mouth was against hers.

She tried to get her arm between them, and to exercise the ju-jitsu trick she had learnt at school, but he knew something of that science. She had seen on entering the room that at one end was a curtained recess, and toward this he was half-lifting, half-carrying her. She did not scream, indeed, to Raphael, she seemed more yielding than he had dared to hope. Twice she tried to speak, and twice he stopped her. She struggled nearer and nearer to the curtained brocade..

The two Italian servants were in the kitchen which was somewhat removed from the room, but they heard the scream and looked at one another, and then with one accord they flew into the hall. The door of the drawing-room was unlocked: they flung it open. Near by the curtain Raphael Willings lay on his face, three inches of Assyrian dagger in his shoulder, and standing by him, staring down at him, was a white-faced girl.

One of the men jerked the dagger from his master's back, and lifted him groaning to a sofa, whilst the other rushed to the telephone. In his agitation the Italian who was endeavouring to staunch the flow of blood from the wound, jabbered unintelligibly at the girl, but she did not hear him, and would not have understood him if she had.

Like one in a dream she walked slowly from the room, through the hall, and into the open.

Raphael Willings's car was drawn up some distance from the front of the house, and the chauffeur had left it unattended.

She looked round; there was nobody in sight; then all her energies awakened, and she sprang into the driver's seat and pressed the plug of the starter. With a whine and a splutter the engines started up, and she sent the car flying down the drive—but here was an obstacle. The iron gates at the end were closed, and she remembered that the chauffeur had had to get down to unlock them. There was no time to be lost. She backed the car, then sent it full speed at the gates. There was a smashing of glass, a crash as the gates broke, and she was in the road with a damaged radiator, lamps twisted beyond recognition, and a mudguard that hung in shreds. But the car was moving, and she set it spinning in the direction of London.

The hall porter of the flats in which she lived did not recognise her, she looked so wild and changed.

"Aren't you well, miss?" he asked as he took her up in the lift.

She shook her head. Once behind the door of her flat she went straight to the telephone and gave a number, and to the man who answered, she poured forth such a wild, incoherent story, a story so punctuated by sobs, that he found it difficult to discover exactly what had happened.

"I'm through, I'm through," she gasped. "I can do no more! I will no do more! It was horrible, horrible!"

She hung up the receiver, and staggered to her room, feeling that she was going to faint unless she took tight hold of herself; hours passed before she was normal.

And it was in that condition that Mr. Derrick Yale found her when he called that evening—her old calm, insolent self.

"This is an unexpected honour," she said coolly, "and who is your friend?"

She looked at the man who was standing behind Yale.

"Thalia Drummond," said Yale sternly. "I have a warrant for your arrest."

"Again?" she raised her eyebrows. "I seem always to be in the hands of the police. What is the charge?"

"Attempted murder," said Yale. "The attempted murder of Mr. Raphael Willings. I caution you that what you now say may be taken down, and used in evidence against you." The second man stepped forward and took her arm.

Thalia Drummond spent that night in the cells of Marylebone Police Station.

CHAPTER XXXIX

"As to what happened, I have yet to learn," said Derrick Yale to a silent but attentive Inspector Parr. "I arrived at Onslow Gardens just after Willings had taken the girl away. The servants at the house were rather reluctant about giving me information, but I soon discovered that she had been taken to Willings's house in the country. Whether she enticed him or he lured her is a matter for discovery. Probably he is under the impression that she went against her will. All along I have suspected Thalia Drummond as being something more than a servant of the Crimson Circle; naturally I was a little alarmed and flew off to Thetfield, arriving at the house just after she had left. She escaped in Willings's car, smashing the lodge gates en route; by the way—that girl has got nerve."

"How is Willings?"

"He will recover; the wound is superficial, but what is significant is the proof that the crime was premeditated. Willings only missed the dagger with which he was stabbed this afternoon, after he had left the girl alone in his armoury whilst he put on his overcoat. He thinks she must have carried it in her muff, and that, of course, is very likely. He gives me no very clear account of what were the events which immediately preceded the stabbing."

"H'm," said Inspector Parr. "What sort of a room was it? I mean, the room where this nearly—occurred?"

"A pretty little drawing-room communicating with what Willings calls his Turkish room. It is a marvellous replica of an Eastern interior, and I should imagine the scene of more or less disreputable happenings—Willings hasn't the best of reputations. It is only separated from the drawing-room by a curtain, and it was near the curtain that he was found."

Mr. Parr was so absorbed in his meditation that his companion thought he had gone to sleep. But the inspector was not asleep; he was very wide awake. He was conscious of the appalling fact that once more whatever kudos attached to the latest of the Crimson

Circle's outrages went to his companion, and yet he did not grudge him the honour.

Without warning he delivered himself of a sentiment which seemed to have no bearing whatever upon the matter they were discussing.

"All great criminals come to grief through trifling errors of judgment," he said oracularly.

Yale smiled. "The error of judgment in this case, I presume, being that they didn't kill our friend Willings—he is not a nice man, and I should imagine of all the members of the Cabinet he could best be spared. But I for one am very grateful that these devils did not get him."

"I am not referring to Mr. Willings," said Inspector Parr rising slowly. "I am referring to a stupid little lie told me by a man who really should have known better."

And with this cryptic utterance, Mr. Parr went off to break the news to Jack Beardmore.

It was typical of him that Jack was the first person who came to his mind when he learnt of Thalia Drummond's arrest. He was fond of the boy, fonder than Jack could guess, and he knew, even better than Yale, how heavily the weight of Thalia Drummond's guilt would lie upon the man who loved her.

Jack had already received his shock. The news of the girl's arrest had been published in the stop-press columns of the late editions, and when Parr arrived he was the picture of desolation.

"She must have the best lawyers procurable," he said quietly. "I don't know that I ought to take you into my confidence, Mr. Parr, because you naturally will be on the other side."

"Naturally," said the inspector, "but I've got a sneaking regard for Thalia Drummond, too."

"You?" said Jack in astonishment. "Why, I thought—"

"I'm human," said the inspector. "A criminal to me is just a criminal. I have no personal grudge against the men I have arrested. Truland, the poisoner, whom I sent to the gallows, was one of the nicest fellows I've ever met, and I got quite fond of him after a bit."

Jack shuddered.

"Don't talk of poisoners and Thalia Drummond in the same breath," he said testily. "Do you honestly believe she is the leading spirit of the Crimson Circle?"

Mr. Parr pursed his thick lips.

"If somebody came to me and told me the Archbishop was the leading light, I shouldn't be surprised, Mr. Beardmore," he said. "By the time this Crimson Circle business is settled, we are all going to have shocks. I started my investigations prepared to believe that anybody might be the Crimson Circle—you, or Marl, the Commissioner or Derrick Yale, Thalia Drummond—almost anybody."

"And you still hold that opinion?" asked Jack with an attempt at a smile. "For the matter of that, Mr. Parr, you yourself might be the villain of the piece."

Mr. Parr did not deny the possibility.

"Mother thinks—" he began, and this time Jack did actually laugh.

"Your grandmother must be a remarkable personality; has she views on the Crimson Circle?"

The inspector nodded vigorously.

"She always has had, since the first murder. She put her finger down on the very spot, Mr. Beardmore, but mother always could do that sort of thing. I've had my best inspirations from her; in fact, all the—" He stopped himself.

Jack was amused, but he was pitying, too. This man, so ill-equipped by nature for his work, had probably won himself a high place in the police service by dogged unimaginative persistence. In every service men had reached near to the top with no other merit than their seniority. It was just a little fantastic at this moment, when the keenest brains were exercised to lay this bizarre association by the heels, to hear this stout man talking solemnly of the advice he had received from his grandmother!

"I must come along and renew my acquaintance with your aunt," said Jack.

"She has gone into the country," was the reply, "and I'm all alone. A woman comes in every morning to clean the place, but there's nobody there evenings—it doesn't seem like home to me now."

It was a relief to Jack to get on to the subject of Mr. Parr's domestic affairs. Their very unimportance was a sedative to his racked mind. He felt that an evening spent with the inspector's knowledgeable grandparent might even restore him to something like normality.

Parr himself led the conversation back to more serious channels.

"Drummond will be brought up to-morrow and remanded," he said.

"Is there any hope of getting bail for her?"

Parr shook his head. "No. She'll have to go to Holloway, but that won't do her much harm," he said, heartlessly, as Jack thought. "It is one of the best prisons in the country, and maybe she'll be glad of the rest."

"How came Yale to arrest her? I should have thought that was your job?"

"I instructed him," said Parr. "He has now the status of a regular police officer, and as he had been in the case earlier in the day, I thought I would let him continue it to the end."

Just as the inspector had foreshadowed, the police-court proceedings of the next day were confined only to evidence of arrest, and Thalia Drummond was remanded in custody.

The court house was packed, and a big crowd, attracted by the sensational character of the charge, filled all the roads approaching the court. Mr. Willings was not well enough to attend, but well enough to send his resignation to the Cabinet in response to the Prime Minister's suggestion, contained in a letter couched in such unpleasant terms—and the acidulated vocabulary of the Prime Minister was notorious—that even he, the thick-skinned Willings, was pained.

Whatever happened, he was everlastingly disgraced; even the thick and thin supporters of his policy would be revolted by the evidence he must give. He had taken the girl—a comparative stranger—to his country house, made violent love to her, and had been stabbed. There could be no romantic version of that unpleasant story; and he heartily cursed himself for his stupidity.

Parr made one call upon the girl whilst she was in prison. She refused to see him in her cell, and insisted upon the interview taking place in the presence of a wardress. She explained her attitude when they sat together in the big gaunt waiting-room of the gaol, he at one end of the table and she at the other.

"You must excuse my not seeing you in my apartment, Mr. Parr," she said, "But so many promising young emissaries of the Crimson Circle have met with an untimely end through interviewing policemen in their cells."

"The only one I can recall," said Parr stolidly, "is Sibly."

"Who was a shining example of indiscretion." She showed her even white teeth in a smile. "Now what do you want of me?"

"I want you to tell me what happened when you called at Onslow Gardens."

She gave him a faithful and a detailed account of that afternoon visit.

"When did you discover the dagger was gone?"

"When I was looking round the room whilst Willings was putting on his coat. How is Lothario?"

"He's all right," said Parr. "I am afraid he will recover—I mean," he added hastily, "I am glad to say he'll get better. Was that the first time Willings noticed the absence of the dagger?"

She nodded.

"Did you carry a muff?"

"Yes," she said. "Is that the place where the deadly weapon was supposed to be concealed?"

"Did you have your muff in your hand when you went into his house at Hatfield?"

She thought a moment. "Yes," she nodded.

Inspector Parr rose.

"You're getting all the food you require?"

"Yes: from prison," she said emphatically. "Prison food will suit me very well, thank you, and I do not want anybody, out of mistaken kindness, to send in luscious dishes from outside, as I understand prisoners on remand are allowed."

He scratched his chin. "I think you're wise," he said.

CHAPTER XL

THE ESCAPE

THE outrage upon Raphael Willings had produced something like a panic in the Cabinet.

Mr. Parr learnt how profound was the concern when he returned to head-quarters. And the Prime Minister was justified in his anxiety. The Crimson Circle had not stated when the next blow would fall, or upon whom.

The inspector was sent for to Downing Street, and was closeted with the Prime Minister for two hours. It was the first personal consultation he had had, and it was followed by a meeting of the inner Cabinet, a fact that was duly recorded in the newspapers.

It was said, but without authority, that the life of the Prime Minister had been threatened, and this statement was neither denied nor affirmed.

Derrick Yale, returning to his flat that night, found Inspector Parr waiting on the door-mat.

"Is anything wrong?" he asked quickly.

"I want your help," said Parr, and did not speak again until he was sitting in a comfortable chair before the fire in Yale's sitting room.

"You know, Yale, that I've got to go, and the Prime Minister is considering the advisability of my going a little sooner than I had expected. There has been a Cabinet committee appointed, and they are calling into question the methods which head-quarters are employing and I have been asked by the Commissioner to attend an informal meeting at the Prime Minister's house to-morrow evening."

"What is the idea?" asked Yale.

"I'm to give a sort of lecture," said Parr gloomily, "and explain to the members of the Cabinet the methods I have employed against the Crimson Circle. You probably know that I have been given unusual powers, and that I have not been asked to tell the Government all I know. I intend doing that on Friday evening, and I want your help."

"My dear chap, you have it before you ask it," said Yale warmly, and Parr went on.

"There is still a lot about the Crimson Circle that is a mystery to me, but I am piecing it together. At the moment I am under the impression that there is somebody at police head-quarters who is working with them."

"That is my view, too," said Yale quickly. "Why do you say that?"

"Well," said the slow Parr, "I'll give you an instance. Young Beardmore had a photograph that he found in his father's papers and this was posted to me. It arrived all right, with the seal of the envelope intact, but when I opened it, there was a blank card. I have since discovered that he gave that card to Thalia Drummond to post; he swears he stood on the doorstep and watched her slip it into the letter-box on the opposite side of the road. If that is the case, the envelope must have been tampered with after it reached head-quarters."

"What kind of a photograph?" asked the other curiously.

"It was either a picture of an execution or the condemned man Lightman, for I think it was taken on the occasion when they tried to execute Lightman and failed. It came to old man Beardmore the day before his death—a great number of things seem to have happened to the victims of the Crimson Circle the day before their death—and was found by Jack and, as I say, sent on—"

"By Thalia Drummond!" said Yale significantly. "My view is that you can exonerate the people at headquarters. This girl is deeper in the Crimson Circle than you imagine. I searched her house to-night—that is where I've been, and this is what I found."

He went out into the hall and returned with a brown paper parcel, opened it, and the inspector stared.

A gauntlet glove and a long bright-bladed knife were exposed when Yale cut the string and stripped away the paper wrapping.

"This glove is a fellow to that which was found in Froyant's study. The knife is an exact pair to the other."

Parr took up the gauntlet and examined it.

"Yes, this is the left hand, and the one on Froyant's desk was the right," he agreed. "It is a worn motor-glove. Who was the owner? Try your psychometric powers, Yale."

"I've already tried," said the other, shaking his head, "but the glove has passed through so many hands that the impressions I receive are very confused. At any rate, this discovery confirms the theory that Thalia Drummond is in the business up to her neck. As to the other matter you were speaking about," he said, as he wrapped the knife and glove carefully in the paper, "I shall be most happy to assist you."

"What I want from you," said Parr, "is that you shall fill in the spaces which I cannot fill," He shook his head. "I only wish Mother could be there," he said regretfully.

"Mother?" said the astonished Yale.

"My grandmother," said Mr. Parr soberly. "The only detective in England—bar you and I."

It was the first time that Derrick Yale ever had reason to suspect that Mr. Parr possessed a sense of humour.

It was typical of that period of excitement, when the name of the Crimson Circle was on every tongue, that sensation should follow sensation. But probably no incident created so much excitement as that which, in scrawling headlines, greeted Derrick Yale as, sitting in bed sipping his tea, he read the newspaper the following morning.

Thalia Drummond had escaped!

People escape from prison in works of fiction; they have been known to make a temporary get-away from dread Dartmoor, but never before in the history of the prison service had a woman escaped from Holloway. And yet the wardress unlocking the door of Thalia Drummond's cell in the morning found it empty.

It took a great deal to shock Derrick Yale, but the news temporarily paralysed him. He read the account of the escape word by word, and in the end he was as mystified as ever.

But there it was in cold print, officially admitted, and communicated to the early morning press by the Government with unnatural haste.

'Owing to the unusual importance of the prisoner, and the character of the offence alleged against her, extraordinary precautions were taken to guard her. The patrol which usually visits the ward in which her cell was situated, was doubled, and instead of hourly, half-hourly visits were paid by the officers on duty. It is not customary to look into every cell on these occasions, but at three o'clock this morning the wardress—Mrs. Hardy—looked through the observation hole and saw the prisoner was there. At six o'clock when the cell door was opened, Drummond was missing. The bars of the window were intact, and the door had not been tampered with.

'A search of the prison grounds showed no trace of her footsteps, and it is almost impossible that she could have escaped over the wall. It is equally impossible that she could have left by the ordinary means, since it would have necessitated her passing through six separate doors, none of which had been forced, or through the gatekeeper's lodge, which is occupied throughout the night.

'This new proof of the Crimson Circle's omnipotence and extraordinary powers is very disconcerting, coming, as it does, at a moment when the lives of Cabinet Ministers are threatened by this mysterious gang.'

Yale glanced at the clock. It was half-past eleven. And then he looked at the newspaper and saw that his servant had brought him an early edition of one of the evening papers. He was out of bed in a second and, not waiting for breakfast, rushed off to head-quarters to find

Inspector Parr in a very good humour, considering all the circumstances.

"But this is incredible, Parr, it is impossible! She must have friends in the prison!"

"That is my idea entirely," said Parr. "I told the Commissioner in the identical words that she must have friends in the prison. Otherwise," he said after a pause, "how did she get out?"

Yale looked at him suspiciously. It did not seem the moment or the occasion for flippant talk, and Inspector Parr's tone was undoubtedly flippant.

CHAPTER XLI

WHO IS THE CRIMSON CIRCLE?

YALE learnt no more details than those he had already read, and took a taxi to his city office, which he had not visited for two days.

The escape of Thalia Drummond was a much more important affair than Parr seemed to think. Parr! An awful thought occurred to Derrick Yale. John Parr! That stolid, stupid-looking man—it was impossible! He shook his head, yet put his mind resolutely to the task of piecing together every incident in which Inspector Parr-had figured, and in the end: "Impossible!" he muttered again, as he walked slowly up the stairs to his office, declining the invitation of the lift-boy.

The first thing he noticed when he unlocked the door was that the letter-box was empty. It was a very large letter-box, with a patent flap device, designed so that it was impossible for an outside pilferer to extract any of its contents. The wire cage reached almost to the floor, and letters that came through the slot in the door had to fall through revolving aluminium blades, which made the letter thief's task a hopeless one. And the letter-box was empty! There was not so much as a tradesman's circular.

He closed the door quietly and went into his own room. He took no more than a pace into the interior and then stopped. Every drawer in his desk was open. The little steel safe by the side of the fireplace, concealed from view by the wooden panelling, had been unlocked and the door was now open. He looked under the desk. There was a tiny cupboard, which only an expert could have found, and here Derrick Yale had kept the more intimate documents connected with the Crimson Circle case.

He saw nothing but a broken panel and the mark of the chisel that had wrenched it free. He sat for a long time in his chair, staring out of the window. There was no need to ask who was the artist. He could guess that. Nevertheless, he made a few perfunctory inquiries, and the lift boy supplied him with all the information he needed.

"Yes, sir, your secretary has been this morning, the pretty young lady. She came in soon after the offices were open. She was only here about an hour, and then she left."

"Did she carry a bag?"

"Yes, sir. A little bag," said the boy.

"Thank you," said Derrick Yale, and went back to head-quarters, to pour into the phlegmatic Mr. Parr's ear a tale of rifled desk and stolen documents.

"Now, I'm going to tell you, Parr, what I have told nobody else, not even the Commissioner," said Yale. "We think of the Crimson Circle organisation as being run by a man. I happen to know that this girl has met the man who initiated her into the mysteries of the gang, whatever they are. But I also know that, so far from being the master, this mysterious gentleman in the motor-car takes his orders, as everybody else does, from the real centre of the organisation—which is Thalia Drummond!"

"Good Lord!" said the inspector.

"You wonder why I had her in my office? I told you it was because I thought she would bring us closer to the Circle. And I was right."

"But why dismiss her?" asked the other quickly.

"Because she had done something which merited dismissal," said Yale, "and if I had not fired her then and there, she would have known that I was keeping her in my office with an object. I might have saved myself the trouble, apparently," he smiled, "because this morning's work proves that she knew what my game was." His thin, delicate face darkened, and then he said almost sharply: "When you have told your story to-night to the Prime Minister and his friends, I have a little story to tell which I think will surprise you."

"Nothing you can say will ever surprise me," said Mr Parr.

The third shock which Derrick Yale received that day came on his return home. The first half of his surprise was to find that his servant was out. The one woman he employed did not sleep on the premises, but she was supposed to remain in the flat until nine o'clock in the evening. It was exactly six when Derrick Yale came in to find the place in darkness.

He turned on the light and made a tour of the rooms.

Apparently, the sitting-room was the only apartment which had been disturbed, but here, whoever the intruder had been—and he could guess her name—she had been very thorough and painstaking. It was not necessary for him to seek out the servant and discover what had happened. She had been called away from the house by a message purporting to come from him—he guessed that much. And whilst she was away Thalia Drummond had examined the contents of the flat at her leisure.

"A clever young woman!" said Derrick without malice, for he could admire even the genius which was employed against himself. She had lost no time. Within twelve hours she had broken gaol, ransacked both his office and his flat, and had removed documents which had a vital bearing upon the Crimson Circle.

He dressed himself leisurely, wondering what would be her next move. Of his own he was certain. Within twenty-four hours Inspector Parr would be a broken man. From a drawer in his dressing-room he took a revolver, looked at it for a moment speculatively, and slipped it into his hip pocket. There was going to be a startling and a sensational end to the chase of the Crimson Circle, an end wholly unforeseen by the spectators of the tragic game.

In the wide lobby of the Prime Minister's house he found a guest, the excuse for whose presence he could not fathom. Jack Beardmore had certainly been a sufferer from the activities of the Crimson Circle, but he had no part in the latter incidents.

"I suppose you are surprised to see me, Mr. Yale," laughed Jack, as he took the other's hand, "but you're not more surprised than I am to be invited to a meeting of the Cabinet." He chuckled.

"Who invited you?—Parr?"

"To be exact, the Prime Minister's secretary. But I think Parr must have had something to do with the invitation. Don't you feel scared in this company?"

"Not very," smiled Derrick, slapping the other on the back.

A youthful private secretary bustled in and ushered them into the severe drawing-room, where a dozen gentlemen were talking in two groups.

The Prime Minister came forward to meet the detective.

"Inspector Parr has not arrived," He looked questioningly at Jack. "I presume this is Mr. Beardmore?" he said. "The inspector particularly asked that you should be present. I suppose he has some light to throw upon poor James Beardmore's death—by the way, your father was a great friend of mine."

The inspector came in at that moment. He wore a dress suit which had seen better days, a low collar with an awkwardly-tied bow, and he seemed an incongruous figure in that atmosphere of intellect and refinement. Following him came the grey-moustached Commissioner, who nodded curtly to his junior and led the Prime Minister aside.

The two were engaged in a whispered conversation for a little time, and then the colonel came across to where Yale was standing with Jack.

"Have you any idea what sort of a lecture Parr is going to give?" he said, a little impatiently. "I was quite under the impression that he was making a statement by invitation, but from what the Prime Minister tells me, it was Parr who suggested he should give the history of the Crimson Circle. I hope he isn't going to make a fool of himself."

"I don't think he will, sir." It was Jack's quiet voice that had interrupted, and the Commissioner looked at him inquiringly until Yale introduced the young man.

"I agree with Mr. Beardmore," said Derrick Yale. "I have not the slightest expectation of Mr. Parr making a fool of himself, in fact, I think he is going to fill up a number of gaps and bridge over seemingly irreconcilable circumstances, and I am ready to fill in a number of spaces which he may leave blank."

The company seated itself, and the Prime Minister beckoned the inspector forward.

"If you don't mind, sir, I'll stay where I am," he said. "I'm not an orator, and I should like to tell this yarn as if I were telling it to any one of you."

He cleared his throat and began speaking. At first his words were hesitant and he paused again and again to find the right phrase, but as he warmed to his subject he spoke more quickly and lucidly.

"The Crimson Circle," he began, "is a man named Lightman, a criminal who committed several murders in France, was condemned to death, but was saved by an accident from execution. His full name is Ferdinand Walter Lightman, and on the date of his attempted execution his age was twenty-three years and four months. He was transported to Cayenne, and escaped from that settlement after murdering a warder, and it is believed got away to Australia. A man answering his description, but giving another name, was working for a storekeeper in Melbourne for eighteen months, and was afterwards in the employment of a squatter named Macdonald for two years and five months. He left Australia in a hurry, a warrant having been issued against him by the local police for attempting to blackmail his employer.

"What happened to him subsequently we have not been able to trace until there appeared in England an unknown and mysterious blackmailer who signed himself the Crimson Circle, and who, by careful organisation and a display of remarkable patience and energy, gathered around him a large number of assistants, all of whom were unknown to one another. His modus operandi—" (the inspector stumbled at the phrase) "—was to find out somebody in a responsible position, who was either in need of money or in fear of prosecution for some offence which he or she had committed. He made the most careful inquiries before he approached his recruit, who was finally interviewed in a closed car driven by the Crimson Circle himself. Usually the rendezvous was one of the London squares which had the advantage of having four or five exits and a further advantage of being poorly lighted; you gentlemen are probably aware that the residential squares of London are the worst illuminated streets in the metropolis.

"Another class of recruit the Crimson Circle was very eager to secure was the convicted criminal. In this way he dragged in Sibly, an ex-sailor of a particularly low intelligence, who was already suspected of having committed murder, and who was the very man for the Crimson Circle's purpose. In this way he secured Thalia Drummond—" he paused—"a thief, and an associate of thieves. In this way, too, he found the black man who murdered the railway director. For his own purpose he put in Brabazon the banker, and would have taken Felix Marl only, unfortunately for Marl, they had been associated together in the very crime for which Lightman nearly lost his life. More unfortunate still, Marl recognised Lightman when he met him in England, and this is the reason why Marl was eventually destroyed, the murderer employing perhaps the most ingenious method that has ever been used by a homicidal criminal.

"You can well understand, gentlemen," he went on. They were following the little man with strained interest. "The Crimson Circle—"

"Why did he call himself Crimson Circle?" It was Derrick Yale who asked the question, and for a little while the inspector was silent.

"He called himself Crimson Circle," he said slowly, "because it was a name he had amongst his fellow convicts. About his neck was a red birth-mark—and I'll blow the top of your head off if you move!"

The heavy calibre Webley he held in his hand covered Derrick Yale.

"Put your hands right up!" said the inspector, and then suddenly he reached out his hand and tore away the high white collar which covered Yale's neck.

There was a gasp. Red, blood-red, as though it were painted by human agency, a circle of crimson ran about the throat of Derrick Yale.

CHAPTER XLII

MOTHER

IN the room three men had mysteriously appeared—the three who had captured Parr's spy two nights before—and in a second Yale was manacled hand and foot. A deft hand jerked the pistol that he carried from his pocket, a third man dropped a cloth bag over his head and face, and he was hurried from the room.

Inspector Parr wiped the perspiration from his streaming forehead, and faced his amazed audience.

"Gentlemen," he said a little shakily, "if you will excuse me for to-night I will tell you the whole of this story to-morrow."

They surrounded him, plying him with questions, but he could only shake his head.

"He's had a very bad time," It was the colonel's voice, "and nobody knows it better than I. I should be very glad, Prime Minister, if you could accede to the inspector's request, and allow the further explanation to stand over until to-morrow."

"Perhaps the inspector will lunch with us," said the Premier, and his Commissioner accepted on Parr's behalf. Gripping Jack's arm Parr marched from the room and into the street. A taxi-cab was awaiting him and he bundled the young man in.

"I feel that I've been dreaming," said Jack when he had found his voice. "Derrick Yale! Impossible! And yet— "

"Oh, it is possible all right," said the inspector with a little laugh,

"Then he and Thalia Drummond were working together?"

"Exactly," was the reply.

"But, inspector, how did you get on to this story?"

"Mother put me on to it," was the unexpected answer. "You don't realise what a clever old lady Mother is. She told me to-night—"

"Then she's come back?"

"Yes, she's come back," said the inspector. "I want you to meet her. She's a bit dogmatic, and she is inclined to argue, but I always let her have her way in that respect."

"And you may be sure I shall, too," laughed Jack, though he did not feel like laughing. "You really believe that the Crimson Circle is in your hands?"

"I am sure of it," said the inspector. "As sure as I'm sitting in this taxi-cab with you, and as sure as I am that Grandmother is the wisest old lady in the world." Jack maintained a silence until they were turning into the avenue.

"Then this means that Thalia is dragged a little lower?" he said quietly. "If this man Yale is, as you believe, the Crimson Circle, he will not spare her."

"I'm certain of that," said the inspector; "but, lord bless you, Mr. Beardmore, why trouble your head about Thalia Drummond?"

"Because I love her, you damned fool!" said Jack savagely, and instantly apologised.

"I know I'm a bit of a fool," the inspector spoke, between gusts of laughter, "but I'm not the only one in London, Mr. Beardmore, believe me. And if you'll take my advice you'll forget that Thalia Drummond ever existed. And if you've got any love to spare, why, give it to Mother!"

Jack was about to say something uncomplimentary about this paragon of a grandmother, but suppressed his desire. The inspector's maisonette was on the first floor, and he went up the stairs ahead, opened the door and stood for a moment in the doorway.

"Hello, Mother," he said. "I've brought Mr. Jack Beardmore to see you." Jack heard an exclamation. "Come in, Mr. Beardmore, come in and meet Mother."

Jack stepped into the room and stood as if he had been shot. Facing him was a smiling girl, a little pale and a little tired looking, but undoubtedly, unless he were mad or dreaming, Thalia Drummond!

She took his outstretched hand in hers and led him to the table, where a meal for three was laid.

"Daddy, you told me you were going to bring the Commissioner," she said reproachfully.

"Daddy?" stammered Jack. "But you told me she was your grandmother."

She patted his hand. "Daddy has developed a sense of humour, which is very distressing," she said. "I'm always called 'Mother' at home, because I've mothered him ever since my own dear mother died. And that story about his grandmother is nonsense, but you must forgive him."

"Your father?" said Jack.

Thalia nodded. "Thalia Drummond Parr, that is my name. Thank goodness, you aren't a crime investigator, or you would have made inquiries and discovered my ghastly secret. Now eat your supper, Mr. Beardmore; I cooked it myself." But Jack could neither eat nor drink until he had learnt more, and she proceeded to enlighten him.

"When the first of the Crimson Circle murders occurred and Daddy was put into the case, I knew that he had a tremendous work in front of him and that the chances were he would fail. Daddy has a lot of enemies at headquarters, and our Commissioner asked him not to take the case, knowing how difficult it was going to be. You see, the Commissioner is my godfather," she added smilingly, "and naturally he takes an interest in our affairs. But Daddy insisted, though I think he regretted it the moment he had taken it on. I have always been interested in police work, and just as soon as Father got behind the Crimson Circle organisation and knew the methods that the Circle employed to gather its recruits, I decided to start upon a career of crime.

"Your father received the first threat three months before it was put into execution. It was two or three days afterwards that I secured a post as secretary to Harvey Froyant, for no other reason than that his estate adjoined yours. He was a friend of your father, and it gave me an opportunity of watching. I tried to get employment with your father. Perhaps you don't know that," she said quietly, "but I failed. Even more dreadful, I was in the wood when he was killed." She squeezed his hand sympathetically. "I didn't see who it was who fired the shot, but I flew forward to where your father was lying, only to discover that he was beyond help, and then, seeing you through the trees running across the meadows toward the wood, I thought I had better get away. The more so," she added, "since I had a revolver in my hand at the time, for I had seen a man stalking in the wood and I had gone in to investigate.

"With the death of your father there was no longer any need for me to remain in the service of Mr. Froyant. I wanted to get closer to the Crimson Circle, and I knew the best way to attract the attention of the man who controlled the gang was for me to embark on a criminal career. It was not providential that you were passing the pawnshop when I came out after pledging Mr. Froyant's golden image. My father manoeuvred that, and when he described me as a thief and an associate of crooks, it was to create an atmosphere, which would impress Derrick Yale, or Ferdinand Walter Lightman, to give him his real name. There was no danger of my being sent to prison. The magistrate treated me as a first offender, but my reputation was gone, and immediately after, as I expected, I received a summons to meet the head of the Crimson Circle.

"I met him one night in Steyne Square. I think Daddy was watching me all the time and shadowed me back to the house. He was never far away, were you, darling?"

"Only at Barnet," he shook his head. "I was scared there, Mother."

"My first task as a member of the Crimson Circle was to go to Brabazon. You see, Yale's method was to set one member to spy upon another. Mr. Brabazon puzzled me. I was never quite sure whether he was straight or crooked, and of course I had no idea at first that he was a member of the gang. I had to begin stealing again in order to sustain my character. It brought down on me a reprimand from my mysterious chief, but it served a useful purpose, for it brought me into contact with a gang of crooks and led unconsciously to my being present in Marisburg Place when Felix Marl also died.

"Yale's object in employing me was to divert suspicion from himself. Besides which, he had intended a very pretty ending to my youthful life. The night he killed Froyant I was ordered to be in the vicinity of the house with a similar knife and the fellow gauntlet to that which Yale used himself in his dreadful crime."

"But how did you escape from prison?" asked Jack.

She looked at him with amusement in her eyes. "You dear boy," she said, "how could I escape from prison? I was let out by the governor in the middle of the night and escorted to my home by a respectable inspector of police!"

"We wanted to force Yale's hand, you see," explained Parr. "As soon as he knew that Mother was out he got rattled and began to hurry his preparations for flight. When he found that his office had been burgled he was pretty sure that Thalia was something more than he had dreamt she was."

CHAPTER XLIII

THE STORY CONTINUED

JACK went to the luncheon party the next day and so, too, did Thalia, who had played such a part, and was the public heroine of the hour. After lunch the inspector completed his story.

"If you take your minds back, gentlemen, you will remember that the name of Derrick Yale had never been heard until the first of the Crimson Circle murders. It is true that he had established himself in a city office, that he had issued circulars, had put advertisements in the paper describing himself as a psychometric detective, but the cases which came to him were very few. Of course, he did not want any cases. He was working up to his big coup. It was after the first murder, you remember, that Derrick Yale was employed by a newspaper, which wanted a good sensational story, to employ his psychometric powers in the tracking of the criminal.

"Who knew better than Yale the name of the murderer and how the murder was committed? You remember that he was able to reconstruct the crime by feeling the weapon with which it was committed. And, in consequence, a black man was arrested, in exactly the spot where Derrick Vale said he would be. Naturally when these facts were disclosed Yale's reputation rose sky-high. It was the very situation that he expected. He knew now that a man threatened by the Crimson Circle would be inclined to call in his assistance, and that is just what happened.

"By being near his victims and gaining their confidence—for Yale was a most convincing type of man—he was able to urge them to pay the demands of the Crimson Circle, and if they refused he was on hand to encompass their death.

"Froyant might not have died, and certainly would not have died at Yale's hands, but for the fact that, annoyed by losing so much money, he made inquiries himself. Starting on a hypothesis which was based upon the faintest suspicion, he worked up the case against Derrick Yale, and was able to identify Lightman and Derrick Yale as one and the same person. On the night of his death he sent for us, intending to make this disclosure, and as a proof that he was in some fear he had two loaded revolvers by his hand, and it is well known that Froyant disliked intensely the employment of firearms.

"And you will remember, if you have read the official minutes of the case, the Commissioner rang up Froyant in response to a call which Harvey Froyant had put through. That call gave Yale his opportunity. It was an excuse for Froyant sending us out of the room. I went first, never dreaming that he would dare do what he did. When we went into the room we wore our overcoats, and I particularly noticed that Derrick Yale kept his hand in his pocket. On the hand, gentlemen," he said impressively, "was a motor-driver's gauntlet, and in that hand was the knife that slew Froyant."

"But why did he wear the glove?" asked the Prime Minister.

"In order that his hand, which I should see immediately afterwards, should not be bloodstained. The moment my back was turned, he lunged straight at Froyant's heart, and Froyant must have died instantly. He slipped off the glove and left it on the table, walked to the door, and seemed to be carrying on a conversation with a man who was already dead.

"I knew this had happened, but I had no proof. He had brought my daughter there, intending to get her into the house, which we immediately searched, with the intention of accusing her of the crime. But she very wisely went no farther than to the back of the house and then, suspecting his plot, went home. But I am anticipating. Amongst the people whom we had to guard was James Beardmore, and James Beardmore was a land speculator, a man who knew all kinds of people, good and bad. That day he was expecting a visit from Marl, whom he had never seen, and he mentioned Marl's name earlier in the day to his son, but not to Derrick Yale. As Marl came toward the house the last person in the world he expected to see was his fellow criminal of Toulouse Gaol, a man whom he had betrayed to his death.

"Derrick Yale must have been standing at the end of the shrubbery, and Marl caught a momentary glimpse of him and went back to the village, ostensibly to London, in a panic of fright, determined, in his fear, that he would kill Lightman before Lightman killed him. His courage must have oozed. He was not a particularly brave man, and instead he wrote a letter to Yale, pushing it under his window—a letter which Yale read and partially burnt. What the letter was I cannot tell you, except it was probably a statement that if he, Marl, was left alone, he would leave Yale alone. He could not have known in what capacity Mr. Derrick Yale was posing. The words 'Block B' undoubtedly referred to the Block at Toulouse Prison.

"From that moment Marl was a doomed man. He was conducting a little blackmail of his own with Brabazon, an agent of the Crimson Circle, and Brabazon must have intimated the danger to Yale who, in his capacity as detective, visited the shop to which all the Crimson Circle letters were addressed, and on the pretext of aiding justice opened them of course and saw their contents, without having the responsibility of being the person to whom they were addressed.

"It was Brabazon's intention to bolt on the day of Marl's murder, and with that object he had cleared out the whole of Marl's balance and had made preparations for flight. On Marl's death suspicion naturally fell upon him and, intimated by the Crimson Circle that he was in danger, he hurried off to the riverside house which we searched."

Detective-Inspector Parr chuckled.

"When I say 'we searched it,' I mean Yale searched it. In other words, he went into the room where he knew Brabazon was, and came down reporting that all was clear."

"There is one point I'd like you to clear up—the chloroforming of Yale in his office," said the Prime Minister.

"That was clever, and deceived me for a moment, Yale handcuffed, strapped and chloroformed himself after he had put the money in an envelope and dropped it down the letter-chute—it was addressed to his private residence. Do you remember, sir, that the postman left the building, having cleared the box, a few minutes after the 'outrage'? Unfortunately for Yale, I had let Thalia into the room and put her into the cupboard, where she witnessed the whole comedy and retrieved the chloroform bottle which he had put into a drawer of his desk."

"The last victim, Mr. Raphael Willings," here Parr spoke very clearly and deliberately, "owes his life to the fact that he conceived an unhealthy attachment for my daughter. She was struggling with him, when, looking over her shoulder, she saw a hand come from behind the curtain holding the very knife that had been stolen earlier in the day by Yale (again in his capacity as detective). It was aimed at Mr. Willings's heart, but by a superhuman effort, she thrust him aside, but not so far as to save him completely. Yale, of course, was on hand to discover the outrage (I should imagine he was very annoyed when he found it was not a murder), and of course he had no difficulty in fixing it upon mother—upon Thalia Drummond Parr.

"Consider the cleverness of his operations!" said Parr admiringly. "He had thrust himself into the front rank of private detectives, so that he was on hand to receive information which was invaluable to him as the Crimson Circle. He was eventually taken to police headquarters—at my suggestion—where the most important documents came under his notice. Some of them were not quite as important as he thought, but it saved Mr. Beardmore's life when Yale had the first handling of a photograph of himself taken a few moments before the abortive execution.

"Now, gentlemen, are there any other points that you wish cleared up? There is one I will clear up which is probably not obscure. Two days ago I told Yale that great criminals are usually brought to their end through ridiculous mistakes. Yale had the effrontery to tell me that he had called at Mr. Willings's house after he had left and that the servants had told him where Thalia and Willings had gone. That alone was sufficient to damn him, because he had not been near Willings's house since the morning, and had arrived at the country place at least an hour before the servants had come."

"The question that disturbs me for the moment," said the Prime Minister, "is what reward we can give to your daughter, Mr. Parr? Your promotion is of course an easy matter to arrange, for there is an assistant-commissionership vacant at this moment; but I don't exactly see what we can do for Miss Drummond, except of course to give her the monetary reward which is due for having brought about the capture of this dangerous criminal."

Then a husky voice spoke. It sounded to Jack as though it were his, and the rest of the people about the table seemed to be under the same impression.

"There is no need to bother about Miss Parr," said this strange voice, that was speaking Jack's thoughts, "we are getting married very soon."

When the buzz of congratulation had subsided, Inspector Parr leant toward his daughter.

"You didn't tell me. Mother," he said reproachfully.

"I didn't even tell him," she said, looking at Jack wonderingly.

"Do you mean to say he hasn't asked you to marry him?" demanded her amazed father.

She shook her head.

"No," she said, "and I haven't told him I would marry him either, but I had a feeling that something like this would happen."

* * * * *

Lightman, or Yale, as he was best known, was an exemplary prisoner. His only complaint against the authorities was that they would not let him smoke on his way to his execution.

"They order these things much better in France," he said to the governor. "Now, the last time I was executed—"

To the chaplain he expressed the warmest interest in Thalia Drummond.

"There is a girl in a million!" he said. "I suppose she will marry young Beardmore—he is a very lucky fellow. Personally, women arouse very little enthusiasm in me, and I ascribe my success in life to this fact. But if I were a marrying man, I think Thalia Drummond would be the very type I should search for."

He liked the chaplain because the padre was a big human man who could talk interestingly on places and things and people, and Derrick Yale had seen most of the fascinating places in the world.

On a grey March morning a man came into his cell and strapped his hands.

Yale looked at him over his shoulder.

"Have you ever heard of M. Pallion? He was a member of your profession."

The executioner did not reply, being by etiquette forbidden to discuss other matters than the prisoner's forgiveness for the deed which was about to be committed.

"You should find out something about Pallion," said Yale, as the procession formed, "and profit by his example. Never drink. Drink was my ruin! If it were not for drink I should not be here!"

This little conceit kept him amused all the way to the scaffold. They slipped the noose about his neck and covered his face with a white cloth, and then the executioner stepped back to the steel lever.

"I hope this rope won't break," said Derrick Yale.

It was the last message from the Crimson Circle.

THE END

LaVergne, TN USA
12 October 2009
160545LV00007B/19/P